ST. MARTIN'S

MINOTAUR

MYSTERIES

A RIDE WITH A DEADLY REPTILE . . .

Red lights flashed behind me. I released my seat belt. I had help behind me. I had help in front of me. I had a snake draped across my legs. . . . The air inside the car was frigid. How fast could a snake bite? How fast could I slow my car and leap out? If he was poisonous, at least I had an army of police to get me to the hospital. Ditto if I broke an important part of my anatomy.

I tensed, then threw caution to the wind. In one movement, I slammed on the brakes and opened my car door. The car was still moving when I rolled off the seat and hit the pavement . . .

"A nicely composed debut with a fine lead character. [Harrison] handles Bretta's matter-of-fact, pervasive sorrow with a generally sure hand."   —*Booklist*

"An interesting cozy that brings modern day Amish life to the forefront . . . Janis Harrison lays out her who-done-it in a fine fashion . . . Bretta is a fascinating protagonist . . . The audience will want Ms. Harrison to foster more novels like ROOTS OF MURDER starring a very admirable heroine."

—*Midwest Book-Review*

ROOTS
of
MURDER

JANIS
HARRISON

St. Martin's Paperbacks

Library of Congress Catalog Card Number: 99-22043

ISBN: 0-312-97500-7

Printed in the United States of America

St. Martin's Press hardcover edition / July 1999
St. Martin's Paperbacks edition / July 2000

10 9 8 7 6 5 4 3 2 1

Lovingly dedicated to my husband, Don,
and our two sons, Brandon and Nicholas.

Dreams do come true.

Acknowledgments

The author would like to express her gratitude to the following:

Robert and Bruce Hadley of Hadley Funeral Home in Windsor, Missouri. The epitome of grace and dignity.

Jerome Wareham and Kent Oberkrom, past and present sheriffs of Henry County, Missouri.

Kelley Ragland, my editor. Your faith and insight have been a true gift.

Lori Pope, my agent, Faith Childs Literary Agency, Inc. Thank you doesn't begin to express my appreciation.

Janice Young Brooks and June Rae Wood. You both give new meaning to the word *friend*.

And finally to all the florists I've had the pleasure of working with over the last twenty-five years:

MAY YOUR ROSES NEVER WILT,
MAY YOUR ARTISTRY BE EVERLASTING,
AND MAY YOUR HOLIDAYS BE SOOTHED
WITH BOWLS OF M&M's CANDIES.

Chapter One

"Death times flowers equals big bucks," murmured Lois. To emphasize her point, she fanned a bundle of greenbacks on the counter next to me.

I stared at the cash but didn't touch it. The phrase "blood money" needled my conscience. Four days ago, on Monday evening, three sixteen-year-old boys drove away from the busy streets of River City for a ride in the country. They'd been killed when their car veered off a curve. Compassion for the surviving families had opened wallets, and my floral business had reaped the benefits.

It was after 7:00 P.M. on Friday. Our part in the preparations for the multiple funeral services was done, but the day had been grueling. Any creative juices flowing through my veins had dried up hours ago. My shop was in a shambles, the coolers stripped bare. In the workroom, festive tails of satin ribbon spiraled from the slotted racks. Cabinet doors hung open. The floor was littered with petals, stem ends, and leaf debris.

I'd waited on each family when they came in to order their floral tributes. I didn't personally know these people, but during those heart-wrenching meetings I'd been privy to melancholy memories, copious weeping, and one full-blown bout of hysteria. Not my own, though I'd come close several times. I was emotionally drained and physically exhausted, especially when I looked at the money. It was a blatant reminder of the day we'd put in, and the bereaved people in River City, Missouri.

Twenty miles northwest of the interstate that links St. Louis to Springfield, River City sprawls across craggy, limestone bluffs on the south bank of the Osage River. With a population of thirty thousand, faces and names often become an impersonal blur of humanity. It takes a tragedy like the deaths of these boys to give citizens a quick reality check. Hearts had been touched, mine included. But then, I was well acquainted with the pain that follows the loss of someone I love.

In a flash of frustration and anger, I grabbed the cash, crammed it into a bank bag, zipped it shut, and flung it in the direction of my office. The bag hit the wall and bounced off a shelf. Four design books and a mug of pens toppled to the floor.

Lois's finely arched eyebrows zoomed up before they settled into a frown. "Bretta Solomon, one. Lois Duncan, zero," she drawled. "Tell me the rules so I can play."

That mad burst of energy had sapped the last of my strength. I slumped in a chair and heaved a sigh. "Being a florist is a helluva career. To earn a living from someone dying makes me think I'm laundering tainted money."

Lois pulled up a chair. In one fluid motion, she sat and crossed her long, youthful legs. Somewhere between forty and sixty, Lois doesn't give away her age by word or deed. Her manner of dress is as flamboyant as her floral designs.

We'd been on our feet for twelve hours straight, yet her makeup was flawless, every dark hair in place. I didn't need a mirror to know I looked as if I'd been dragged through a rat hole backwards.

Lois toyed with the gold chain that circled her neck. "I admit funeral work is our bread and butter, but what about the weddings, anniversaries, and hospital orders? Correct me if I'm wrong, but you didn't mind taking Mrs. Hanover's money when she splurged on a Hawaiian theme for her husband's eightieth birthday."

"That's different . . ." I began.

Lois interrupted. "I don't see how. Ethel Hanover was riding high on emotion." She grinned. "What a party. No one on the guest list was under seventy. Brightly flowered muumuus on wizened bodies. Hair so sparse you couldn't pin a hibiscus blossom in it. I heard old Mrs. Hanover ask three different men if they'd like a good 'lei,' then cackle like a hen in heat as she put the garlands around their necks."

"Hens don't come into heat," I corrected my citified friend before returning to the main topic. "Mrs. Hanover was fired up with excitement when she spent her money. These families and friends are moved by grief."

"That's my point, Bretta. Whatever the emotion, people say it with flowers. Happy. Sad. We're here to perform a service. And if I do say so myself, we do a damned fine job."

"I suppose," I murmured, then asked, "Did I tell you I grew up down the road from where the boys were killed? I thought everyone knew that curve is a bitch. That you have to slow down." Bitterly, I added, "Life bites, but death sucks."

Lois shrugged. "True, but you can't have one without the other." She waved her hands. "Life . . . death. That's what it's all about."

"But these boys haven't lived," I persisted. I should have dropped the subject and gone home. But once Lois and I parted ways, I'd be alone. She had her husband, Noah, to hash over the day's events. My husband, Carl, had died fifteen months ago.

I ignored the sharp ache in my chest that always accompanied thoughts of Carl. That ache had throbbed all day until I wondered if I was flirting with a heart attack.

"It's a damned shame," said Lois, "but what's really going on?" She studied me pensively. "Bretta, we've weathered every kind of tragedy known to man in this town. We've done our job, put it behind us, and moved on to the next. Something else is bothering you. What is it?"

How do you explain loneliness to a woman whose house is like a bus depot? Who still has her husband and three of her five children living at home? I didn't have the energy to try. "Forget it," I said, pasting a smile on my lips. "Chalk my mood up to a lack of calories.

It's been months since I tasted anything decadent."

Lois slapped her knees. "Is that all it'll take to bring you out of this royal blue funk?"

Before I could answer, she galloped off. I shrugged. Why not? I knew Lois kept a cache of goodies somewhere in the shop. She ate her treats when I was out or otherwise occupied. But I'd seen the Snickers wrappers in the trash. I'd smelled the peanuts on her breath.

Real chocolate, not the fake kind, hadn't crossed my lips in weeks. In the past fifteen months I'd dieted away one hundred pounds of fat, flab, and dimpled flesh.

From the workroom, Lois called, "I don't want to be accused of contributing to the delinquency of a dieter, but if you're serious, come and get it."

Wearily, I dragged my creaky, forty-five-year-old body toward her voice. Before I could say Hershey, Pennsylvania, Lois produced a pile of illicit sweets. A sack of M&M's appeared from behind the stock of hot glue sticks. Snickers, Milky Ways, and chocolate kisses tumbled out of the canister where we kept the satin corsage leaves.

The tightness in my chest eased and laughter bubbled past the knot in my throat. Encouraged, Lois pulled away the rack of satin ribbon and revealed my impending downfall. Two DoveBars in their pristine blue and silver wrappers.

"You're wicked," I said, grabbing up a bar and peeling away the tinfoil. The chocolate candy was on its way to my mouth when I caught my reflection in the glass flower-cooler door. My image was distorted, but it was a slender image. An image I'd worked damned hard to achieve.

I laid the sweet treat down and put my hands at the indentation of my waist. Never a size six but not a size twenty-six either. Carl had always said there was a slender woman inside of me, and someday I'd let her out. It bothered me that I'd waited till he was dead before proving him right.

I moved closer to the cooler door. Lines of fatigue etched my blue eyes. Short hair showed more gray than brown. Maybe I should color it, go for blond. Try life as a voluptuous redhead. I pressed my hands under my breasts and watched the material of my blouse swell seductively.

Across the room, Lois chuckled. I dropped my boobs and they bounced into their customary place. Glancing over my shoulder, I demanded, "What's so funny?"

"You're like a kid with a new toy. Trouble is, you're hoarding it." She waggled her eyebrows. "Didn't your mama teach you it's better to share?"

I snorted. "Sex doesn't solve everything." I looked at the DoveBar on the table. Losing weight had been a battle. Keeping it off was proving to be a war of wills. I took a deep, soul-cleansing breath and tried to sound confident. "And neither does chocolate."

Lois popped a handful of M&M's into her mouth. She closed her eyes and chewed blissfully. "Maybe not, but it sure does make life more tolerable—and a helluva lot sweeter."

• • •

Carl and I had celebrated twenty-four anniversaries, but a hundred wouldn't have been enough. When I married a cop, I knew I might be a widow sooner than most. With people killing people, cops were always a target. But Carl had died of a heart attack.

I stood in my house at the locked door of the master suite. I hadn't entered the room since he died. Lois knew everything about my life . . . except this. No one knew that fifteen months later I still slept in the guest room, or that my happy memories of Carl were bound around my heart with chains of guilt.

I pressed my fingertips to the wooden panel. The time was coming when I'd have to unlock this door and face the room and its memories. "But not tonight," I muttered. "Borderline depression. Snap out of it."

Making the adjustment from being half of a loving, happy couple to a content, if occasionally lonely, woman hadn't been easy. Evenings were the worst. I'd discovered that having a verbal conversation with myself didn't make me crazy. Fact is, I'd learned several things that kept me on that narrow ledge called sanity.

I plodded through the house, switched the radio to an oldies station, then stepped out on the front porch for the evening paper.

The *River City Daily* was wedged between the spindles of the porch railing. For some unknown reason, the paperboy derived some perverse pleasure from making me work for my news. After a couple of tugs, the roll came free. I stomped into the house and snapped open the paper. The headline speared me between the eyes:

"Good Lord," I murmured as I scanned the skimpy paragraph:

Spencer County authorities are awaiting the results of the coroner's findings in the suspicious death of an Amish man. Thirty-four-year-old Isaac Miller, who grew flowers for the local floral trade, was found late Thursday evening at his home, two miles west of Woodgrove.

I leaned weakly against the door. Tears filled my eyes as I thought of Isaac. He'd been a quiet, reserved man. I brushed a hand wearily across my eyes. What had happened?

Coroner's findings? That meant autopsy. How had Isaac died? I skimmed the article again, hoping for answers. "Too vague," I muttered. The paper said "suspicious death." One word strayed into my mind, but I heard Carl's voice in my ear, "Don't jump the gun, Babe. Accidents happen on farms every day."

That was true. Isaac could have fallen out of the barn loft or a horse could have kicked him. I smiled ruefully. My husband had been a damned fine deputy. I'd helped him with some of his investigations by listening, asking questions, opening up different avenues of thought. He, in turn, had trusted me enough to share this important part of his life with me.

I glanced back at the paper. Suicide? I shuddered.

Isaac and suicide were as incomprehensible as three teenage boys lying in their caskets.

Isaac's flowers were prime quality, cut fresh from his own cultivated gardens. They were a hot item sought by all five of my competitors. I'd been smug when I'd first heard Isaac's plan to grow flowers. I figured I'd have an inside track because Evan Miller, Isaac's brother, had bought my family's farm.

It hadn't worked out that way. Isaac had opted to sell directly to J. W. Moth, owner of River City Wholesale Floral Company. For an Amish man, this made sense. Instead of haggling with a bunch of greedy florists, Isaac's business contact with the outside world was through one man.

I'd been disappointed, but I did get my weekly share of Isaac's product. Occasionally, some of the florists grumble that the division isn't fair—the most vocal being Allison Thorpe, who's the town's biggest agitator since the first washing machine. We'd had a blowup last Valentine's Day over a missing shipment of roses. The woman had accused me—

The shrill ring of the telephone interrupted my thoughts. I picked up the receiver and said, "Hello?"

"Bretta?" came the hesitant male voice.

He sounded familiar. "Yes," I replied, "This is Bretta Solomon."

His voice boomed into my ear. "Evan Miller."

I moved the phone two inches away. The old order Amish don't have phones in their homes, and they rarely use them. I knew Evan disliked making calls, but I figured he wanted to tell me about Isaac. Hoping to spare him this painful task, I said, "Oh, Evan, I just read about Isaac. I'm so sorry."

He offered no verbal comment on his emotions or on his brother's death. Instead, he asked, "Can you come to the farm in the morning? Early. Seven, eight o'clock." A note of caution entered his voice. "I need your . . . advice."

"Advice?"

"Yeah. Uh . . . assistance. Uh . . . about . . ." His tone grew strong again. "The flowers. Isaac's flowers."

"I don't know what kind of assistance I can offer."

"Will you come?" persisted Evan.

"Of course, but—"

"Have to get back to the house. See you in the morning." And *click,* he was gone.

Slowly, I returned the receiver to its niche. I could speculate on what Evan wanted, but I still wouldn't be any wiser until tomorrow morning.

As I bathed and got ready for bed, my mind was on Evan. His summons for assistance from a non-Amish might seem odd, except we had a unique friendship. If Evan had questions and no one in his Amish community had answers, he'd call on me.

I turned off the light and stretched out in my bed. My thoughts jumped and jiggled like drops of water in hot grease. I punched the pillow and tried to relax. Eighteen miles from River City, the small town of Woodgrove had seen an influx of Amish families in the last twenty years. I worked hard at picturing the quaint town, so I could relax and get some sleep, but other images intruded. The most persistent one was Cecil Bellows.

Cecil lives on the gravel road that backs Evan's property. I slugged my pillow again. Thoughts of Cecil were not conducive to a peaceful sleep. He was an obstinate and prejudicial man. I flopped over on my stomach. When I sold my farm to an Amish man, Cecil had been livid.

On the verge of sleep, my mind drew a parallel. The paperboy tossing the newspaper in the shrubs. Wedging it in the porch railing. Leaving it under the downspout during a rainstorm. I'd gotten that same perverse pleasure out of riling Cecil Bellows. I simply didn't like the man.

My eyes popped open. "Well, I'll be damned," I sputtered. "That kid doesn't like me." I kicked the wadded covers off my legs. "What the hell isn't there to like?"

Chapter Two

It was after six the next morning when I left River City. The sky in the east was a vibrant, lavish display of copper, apricot, and gold. Like a prima donna actor, the sun couldn't resist delivering a preview of the talent it would unleash during its daily performance.

I rolled down my window and let the crisp morning air circulate around me. I loved this time of year, the transition from one season to another. September in the Missouri Ozarks has the appearance of an over-the-hill prostitute trying for one last trick before retiring. The blistering days of summer have sapped the freshness of spring. Fall brings rejuvenating showers and another bawdy attempt at youth. The rains hadn't arrived yet, so the landscape was shopworn, tattered around the edges.

These days I rarely make it outside the city limits, so I was eager for the familiar sight of hills rolling into valleys and the tree-covered mountains standing guard in the distance. There's an old maxim about time, smelling, and flowers. Considering my line of work, I, more than most, should have taken it to heart.

The passing of my car rustled drying cornstalks and made them whisper restlessly. Milo was turning from green to bronze. Soybean fields were gaining maturity, the pods plump with seed, tantalizing some hopeful farmer with their promise of a good crop.

The first steering wheel I'd ever held in my hands had been that of a tractor. I'd smelled the muskiness of freshly turned earth. I'd walked barefoot in fields, breaking clods with my toes.

A thickening in my throat told me I was ripe for that twist in the gut nostalgia can bring. I swallowed, then carefully peeled away the bandage that covered a tender area of my childhood.

My father had packed up and moved out when I was eight years old. I'd been young enough to miss him but not old enough to understand why he'd left me. He hadn't liked farming. Hadn't liked the hard work with the small payoff in the end. He'd gone to Texas, where he'd perfected some gizmo that brands cattle without any fuss or muss. As I was growing up, it hadn't helped my self-esteem to know that my father preferred easing the pain of a bunch of cows over me.

When Mom was alive, I'd heard from Dad in the form of a yearly check. After Mom died, Dad's correspondence increased to a card on my birthday and a box of grapefruit at Christmas.

I dashed a hand across my eyes and let the bandage fall back into place. It bothered me that I was still vulnerable to these memories. That after all these years the wound remained sensitive and couldn't take a gentle probing.

I came to the turnoff for Woodgrove, but since I was early, I bypassed the town, taking the scenic route to Evan's place. A county-maintained road, it wasn't as smooth as the state highway, but it offered breathtaking vistas.

Flat cropland gave way to deep ravines and sharp bends in the road. I drove along a ridge that rimmed the valley below. The sun stole a peek over the horizon to make sure its audience was primed and ready. Mists rose from the floor of the hollow like nervous stage-hands. They hovered in the air counting the minutes until showtime. Playful shadows had neglected their duties through the night. With the curtain about to go up, they darted here and there among the trees seeing to final details.

Then, without further ado, the sun materialized in all its glory. Its presence eclipsed the other actors on-stage. The wisps of fog vanished. The shadows dissolved, and the countryside was spotlighted with brilliance.

Farmsteads, nestled among the hills, were a backdrop to the drama that was unfolding. The feathery tips of the buffalo grass, growing along the side of the road, nodded in appreciation. Birds chirped their cheery lines. Insects buzzed with excitement at the prospect of a good review. I crossed a bridge and heard the stream gurgle importantly. It was leaving this production and was moving on to bigger and better things.

I sat up straight in my seat. I'd chosen this route for another reason than its beauty. The scene of the boys' car accident was around the next curve. I took my foot off the gas and coasted down the hill.

On my right, trees grew as thick as hairs on a dog's back. Suddenly, I saw a break. This was the place. I pulled as far off the road as I could and gazed in dismay.

The recently sheared-off trees and mangled underbrush were withered. The fatal path was as wide as a car and plunged down an embankment. The car must have flipped over a gully or sailed brazenly across it, landing against a tree on the far side. A permanent gash on the trunk marked the spot.

Across the road from the accident was Sam Kramer's land. A rusty snarl of barbed wire signaled this dilapidated fence as his property. After my father had left Mom and me, Sam had farmed our property on shares. For two years, his slipshod methods had been an aggravation. Mom had gently eased us out of that arrangement, and for the next ten years, Cecil Bellows had farmed our land.

I gave the accident scene one last look, then drove on, taking two more curves before Evan's house came into view. I'd just left the scene of one tragedy. Now, I faced another. Isaac's wife, Rosalie, is pregnant with her second child. Regardless of how Isaac had died, these people were in the early stages of grief. I knew full well what Rosalie was experiencing. Carl's death had produced a range of responses in me. Denial had come first.

I couldn't believe my husband was truly gone. Discord soon followed, as I was forced to move on in a world that seemed apathetic to my pain. And finally, there had been the harsh reality of acceptance. My life was never going to be the same.

I parked my car under a shade tree, then sat quietly for a few moments. I let the familiar surroundings of my childhood soothe my turbulent emotions. The place looked almost like home. The white clapboard house stood two stories high and had a wraparound porch on three sides. The one jarring note was the lack of my mother's white lace curtains. The nine-room house boasted fifteen windows, all glaringly bare.

A host of young faces peeked out at me. I waved, then grinned as they ducked bashfully out of sight. Chuckling, I got out of the car and saw Evan Miller coming toward me from the barn.

He's tall and lean, his muscles honed from hard physical labor. Lois would have described Evan as "a fine figure of a man." Watching him approach, I had to agree. His Amish clothes were neat and clean, the shirt bright white, the dark trousers held in place by suspenders. A wide-brimmed straw hat sat squarely on his head. A wiry black beard covered his jaws, but his upper lip was shaved clean.

When Cecil farmed our property, he'd acted as if he owned the land. He'd ripped out fences without permission, dug the creekbed deeper, and pastured cows where Mom had distinctly said no livestock. She'd been at her wit's end when Evan came along.

He and Cleome had moved to Woodgrove from Illinois. They'd lived in town, but Evan wanted to farm. He couldn't afford to buy a place of his own, so he'd approached Mom with the hopes of renting her land. She'd liked him, liked the way he carefully explained what he had in mind and which crops he wanted to plant. They'd come to an agreement, and Mom had told Cecil his services were no longer needed.

I hadn't been around for that conversation, and probably it was just as well. By this time I was happily married to Carl and living in River City. I'd bought the flower shop. My life was full. When Mom died, I didn't hesitate selling the farm to Evan. She would've approved of my decision. Evan had moved his family into the farmhouse, and I'd been relieved to know that my homeplace was in caring, loving hands.

I knew Evan to be forty-two, and that he'd been married to Cleome long enough to have produced seven children. When I first met Evan, he and Cleome had Emily and Jacob. In the intervening years, Matthew, Mark, Katie, Luke, and John had been born. No Sabrina, Aurora, or Britton here.

I closed the distance between us and shook Evan's callused hand. "I'm sorry about Isaac," I said.

"Bretta?" he asked uncertainly.

I nodded. Last time I'd seen him, I'd brought practical Christmas gifts to his family. That had been many pounds ago. "Yes. It's been a while. I wish we weren't meeting under such sad circumstances."

"I wouldn't have known you if you hadn't been driving the same car."

"Still me," I said. "Just not as much."

He peered worriedly at me. "You aren't...you haven't been sick?"

I assured him I was healthier than ever. "How about you? Are you okay?"

He lifted a shoulder. "I suppose. Thanks for coming." He grimaced. "To get you here I had to use that phone of Sam's."

I grinned. "It has its uses."

"Yeah. Yeah," he muttered.

Normally, we'd slip into an easy conversation about the weather or the crops. But what followed instead was that uncomfortable silence that comes when two people have something to say and neither knows how to begin. I wanted to ask about Isaac's death, but there's a way to approach Evan, and it isn't to blurt out questions. I had to ease into it gently. I tried to prod him along.

"I'm not sure what help I'll be. About all I can do is arrange Isaac's flowers into a bouquet that would knock your socks off." I glanced quickly at his boots. I'd never had reason to see Evan's feet. Did Amish men wear socks?

Evan saw where my eyes had traveled and guessed my thoughts. He gave me one of his rare smiles. It showed amusement, but spoiled his looks because he was missing a front tooth. Dentistry isn't high on an Amish man's list of necessities. If it don't hurt, don't fix it.

Embarrassed, I labored on. "If you want to talk to me about growing the flowers—"

"No, no," he hastened to say. "Not that. No."

"Then I don't—"

The creak of the back door caused us to turn. Cleome and her daughter, Katie, stepped from the house. "Hi," I called. When they didn't respond, I thought they didn't recognize me. I added, "It's me, Bretta."

Cleome hesitated, then dipped her head in a sharp nod. She spoke to Katie. They stepped off the porch and crossed the yard. The Amish woman's spine was as stiff and unyielding as a hickory stick. She disappeared around the corner of the house. Katie, right behind her, looked back at me. Down at her side, her fingers wiggled the tiniest of greetings, then she was gone.

Puzzled, I turned to Evan. "Chilly around here, isn't it?"

He understood what I meant. I'd never seen him disconcerted. His convictions kept him on a path his faith decreed was ordained by God. He shuffled his heavy work boots in the dust, hemmed and hawed, and wouldn't meet my direct gaze.

By now I was totally confused. "Cleome's greeting just missed being a snub," I said. "Why? You invited me to come here."

"I want to show you something." He led the way around the house, where I saw Cleome and Katie working in the garden. At our approach, Katie looked up, but Cleome hoed the ground harder. She said something in a curt tone, and Katie obediently bent back to her task.

A few steps ahead of me, Evan walked rapidly past the garden. I glanced over my shoulder and saw Cleome had stopped attacking the dirt. Her hands gripped the hoe handle, and her eyes drilled into me.

A strange, difficult woman, Cleome had always been cordial in the past. However, our conversations were often stilted. I didn't have children. She had seven. I wasn't much of a cook. Her meals were executed with precision. I couldn't sew a seam if my life depended on it. She made all her family's clothes. We had nothing in common. Isaac had been like Cleome—a private person, keeping his thoughts to himself. I hadn't been able to talk to him as I could Evan. Evan and I have been known to jabber for hours. Livestock. Market prices. Tilling the south field. Rotating crops. But today Evan was unusually silent on *all* subjects.

He didn't slow as we approached Isaac's house. We breezed by it, another vegetable garden, a clothesline full of towels and sheets, a compost pile, and a shed filled with horse-drawn farm machinery.

None of these buildings had existed when I owned the property. The changes had been made after Isaac and Rosalie moved here from Pennsylvania. But I clearly hadn't been brought out here for a tour, so I tried again. "Look, Evan, I—"

He stopped abruptly, and I nearly rammed my nose into his broad back. My feet skidded on the gravel as I did some fancy dance steps to keep my balance. If Evan noticed my ungainly performance, he made no sign. His eyes were on something else, his lips pressed into a grim line.

I followed his gaze and saw Isaac's field of flowers. Two acres in full-blown color, grown by a man who had been truly dedicated to his work.

Drawn to the exquisite display, I walked closer. I barely noticed Isaac's greenhouse and the holding shed where he'd kept the cut flowers until they were trucked into River City. My attention was on the field.

Clouds of white baby's breath billowed in the breeze, an airy, ethereal background to the other blossoms. Bright carmine asters. Celosia with orange, scarlet, and golden yellow plumes. Burnished cosmos. Zinnias. Statice. A mass of vibrant blue cornflowers struck a brilliant contrast and rivaled the sky with their color.

My fingers itched to touch these beauties, to stroke the velvet petals and smell the mixed aromas, but a movement farther up the hill killed my artistic desires. A sheriff's deputy leaned against a tree.

"What's he doing?" I asked.

Evan's mouth turned down. "You'd have to ask the sheriff."

"How long has he been there?"

"The men change, but someone has been up there since Thursday night. After Isaac died."

A guard? In Isaac's flower field? Gently, I said, "The newspaper didn't give any details about Isaac's death. What happened?"

Evan jerked his head toward the colorful array. "My

21

brother died up there among his flowers."

"What was he doing?"

"Cutting flowers for market."

I tried to think of what might have happened. "Was he using a wagon? Did the horse bolt?"

Evan grinned weakly. "Old Jake doesn't have the energy to run." He sobered and his fingers skittered over his wiry beard. "I don't always understand your English laws, Bretta. Why an autopsy? What are they looking for?"

Was this possibly murder? But what if I was misreading the sketchy information? Playing it safe, I hedged, "A detail about Isaac's death must not have set well with the coroner. What was said to you?"

He snorted his frustration. "All I get is questions without answers."

"What kind of questions?"

Evan flapped his hands impatiently. "Did Isaac have any enemies? No. Did my brother take a nip or two on the side? No. Did my brother and I quarrel?" His voice rose in outrage. "Absolutely not."

With an effort, he calmed down. "I called you, Bretta, because I trust you. I want you to find out what's going on. I want to know when we can have Isaac's body back. Our people are nearly finished with the coffin. The grave is being dug. He's already in God's hands. It's up to us, his family, to finish our earthly duty."

"Evan, I'm a florist. I can't do anything about Isaac's body. When the coroner is finished with his examination, the body will be released to the funeral home. I'm sure Margaret will bring Isaac home as soon as she can."

Margaret Jenkins owns Woodgrove's only funeral home. I knew the Amish counted this older woman as a friend. She'd made herself indispensable to the Amish colony around Woodgrove by taking them in her car to doctor appointments or other errands too far away to be reached with a horse and buggy. I offered her name to Evan, hoping he'd take comfort in it. I held out my hands helplessly. "Until then, there's nothing anyone can do but wait."

Evan sighed. "I just don't understand."

"Maybe if you told me what happened," I prompted.

Reluctantly, without emotion, Evan related the events of his brother's death. He recited the facts in a monotone, as if he'd repeated this story a dozen times.

"Isaac and I'd been at a farm sale Thursday afternoon. We got home late, and Isaac still had flowers to cut for pickup the next day. I offered to help, but he said he needed to think. Since I had my own chores to do, I left him hitching up Old Jake to the wagon so he could collect the flowers."

"What did he need to think about? Was there something specific on his mind?"

"Not that I know. He was always reading books, going to the library."

"So you were at the barn, and Isaac was alone in the field?"

He gave me a quick look. "Isaac wasn't alone all the time. But that's getting ahead of the story."

Isaac in the field. Isaac not alone. Isaac dead. The

nasty picture was coming into focus, but I pressed my lips together and let him talk.

"I had finished the chores and was washing up for supper when Amelia, Isaac's daughter, came to the house for help. Her mother had found Jake still hitched to the wagon outside the holding shed, but Isaac wasn't inside. The cans of water had been overturned, the flowers ruined."

Evan's stoical composure cracked. He mopped his damp face with a handkerchief. "Rosalie didn't wait for me. She went to the field and found Isaac. He was dead."

Evan fingered the fastener of his suspenders. "I will apologize for Cleome. She's upset because I called you. She thinks I'm stirring up trouble. The way I see it, the stirring has already been done. Cleome says, let it rest, bury our dead and continue with God's plan."

"The sheriff might have something to say to that."

"The sheriff is a *gröt rŏs sprecha.*"

The Amish speak a combination of High German and Pennsylvania Dutch. I didn't understand the phrase Evan used, but I knew Sid Hancock, sheriff of Spencer County. Sid is abrupt and relentless, maybe a good combination for a lawman, but lousy if you're on the other end of his interrogations.

Sid and I'd gotten off on the wrong foot not long after he'd been elected sheriff. Carl had come home one evening thoroughly frustrated with a case he was working on. The county was being plagued by a rash of petty robberies. No leads. No witnesses. The pilfering covered all four corners of the county. Nothing major was taken: small appliances, feather pillows, silk flower arrangements, Tupperware, baskets, stuffed toys, and other odds and ends.

I'd laughed and said maybe the deputies needed to attend some local garage sales. Carl had passed on my suggestion to Sid. They'd acted on it and the robbers, a woman and her three daughters, had been apprehended.

Carl had been interviewed by a reporter from the *River City Daily*. Like the kind and loving husband he'd been, he proudly included me in the success of the bust. The paper gobbled up this tidbit and spit out a front-page tale that made me sound like I was the next Nancy Drew of River City. Sid had been furious. He'd wanted the limelight kept on his office, not transferred to the wife of one of his officers.

Since that fiasco, I tread lightly around Sid. I didn't want to think about him and what his reaction would be when he heard that Evan had summoned me to the farm. A glance at the deputy left me with little doubt that Sid would hear. On the other hand, my friendship with the Amish, especially Evan, is no secret.

"Did you tell the sheriff about someone being in the field with Isaac?" I asked.

"No" was Evan's terse reply. "I don't want that man questioning my Katie."

"Katie?" This news hit me broadside. The thought of Katie having seen something sinister made my skin crawl with bumps of apprehension. My favorite among Evan's children, nine-year-old Katie is as fresh and innocent as a shasta daisy. "What's she got to do with this?"

"Nothing," snapped Evan, "and that's the way I want it. I saw no one. No car pulled into the drive. Rosalie didn't see anyone. No one came to either house."

His wide shoulders slumped as if he'd taken on the weight of the world. With a dazed expression, he continued quietly, "Katie says that she saw someone in the field. My brother is dead, but no one has admitted to being with him before he died." Evan's voice dropped to a hoarse whisper. "Why not admit to being with Isaac that evening? Why keep it a secret?"

His eyes caught mine in a pain-filled gaze. He answered his own question. "Unless something wicked happened. Something so terrible that the person has to hide it."

I took a deep breath, as if to make a lengthy speech, but I said only one word. "Murder."

Evan's lean frame shuddered. Our heads turned in unison to the flower field. The blossoms were a lovely memorial to Isaac's short life.

"Did Katie recognize—" Before I could get the words out, a scream of terror ripped the air.

"That's Cleome," shouted Evan, taking off at a run.

Chapter Three

I followed Evan around the buildings and saw Cleome in the garden trying to keep an aggressive billy goat at bay with her hoe. The goat was black and white with lethal-looking horns curled up and over his head. Using the hoe, Cleome nudged the animal. Instead of retreating, he pawed the loose soil, lowered his head, and took a bold step in her direction. Her mouth stretched wide, and she erupted with another ear-shattering scream.

Evan reached the garden, pressed his hands on top of the woven-wire fence, and vaulted over. "Shoo! You old rover," he shouted.

This goat was no fool. He might intimidate a woman, but Evan was another matter. The goat gave us a superior look, then, as graceful as a deer, he leaped the fence, sauntered across the yard and up the middle of the blacktop highway.

Cleome followed his retreat with fire in her eyes. Her hands rested on her hips; her weapon lay at her bare feet. A bundle of energy, Cleome Miller was short in stature but stood tall in her faith. She had a round face, plump cheeks, and sharp, intelligent eyes. Her stomach was pudgy and misshapen from bearing one child right after another and another.

She clucked her tongue before saying, "Our cats and dogs are killed on this road, but that old goat can come and go as he pleases without harm ever approaching a hair on his mangy hide."

"Sam Kramer?" I asked.

Cleome grimaced. "Some things never change. It's a good thing Isaac didn't see——" Her voice trailed off. She struggled for composure. Evan took a step in her direction, but she raised her chin and squared her shoulders. When she spoke, it was back to more mundane things. "I have bread in the oven."

Carrying her hoe, she walked briskly between the neat rows of vegetables. At the end, she hung the hoe on the garden gate and hurried to the house.

As soon as I heard the door shut, I asked Evan, "What did she mean about Isaac?"

"Sam and Isaac had an ongoing feud. The goat has been a constant worry for Isaac. We've tried talking to Sam, but he says someone is letting the goat out of his pen to cause trouble."

"Why would anyone do that?"

"I don't know that they are. That's Sam's story. Isaac and I talked about fencing off the flower field." Evan nodded to the wire enclosure. "But you saw how well that works."

I was about to say Sam was a harmless, if eccentric, old man when a red pickup truck barreled into the driveway. Under his breath, Evan muttered something, then ducked his head as if embarrassed.

I could guess at his words because I recognized the driver. "Cecil Bellows making a neighborly call?" I asked.

"Call? Yes. Neighborly? No," replied Evan as he picked his way out of the garden. He propped the gate shut with the hoe, then we walked toward the truck.

Edna, Cecil's wife, caught sight of us and timidly raised her hand. She got out of the truck when she saw Cleome standing on the porch.

From inside the cab, Cecil said, "Well, woman, get on with it. I have work to do."

Edna lifted a covered dish from the seat and hurried across the yard to Cleome. "I won't bother Rosalie, but I wanted her to have this casserole."

In the olden days, Edna Bellows had been my mother's best friend. Mom had said Edna was like a little brown wren, tending her nest, raising her brood, looking after the neighbors. According to my mother, Cecil, on the other hand, was a buzzard. That said it all.

Today, Edna was properly dressed for a condolence call. Brown skirt, tan blouse, sensible shoes and hose. There was just the right note of sympathy in her voice. No probing questions. No awkward tears.

As I started toward her, Cecil leaned on the truck's horn. Above the roar of the engine, he yelled, "I said to hurry, Edna. I gotta pick up a tractor part."

From the perch of his four-wheel-drive machine,

Cecil smirked down at Evan. "Miller, you people might have the right idea using horses. You don't have time to go all over the country making useless social calls."

Evan was too kind to comment. "Reticent" could never be used to describe me. I stepped forward. "I see your manners haven't improved."

Cecil leaned out his window to give me a long, hard look. "Bretta McGinness," he said, calling me by my maiden name. "Well, I'll be damned. I'd know that voice anywhere, though you look like your throat's been cut." I stiffened at the snide reference to my recent weight loss. "Same disrespect for your elders," he continued. "I always told your mother that she let you get away with too much. If you'd been my kid, you'd have—"

"—moved five states away," I filled in dryly. That was what his three children had done.

Cecil's eyes narrowed. "Always too big"—he gave a rude guffaw of laughter—"and I mean *big* for your britches. Your body may be smaller, but your mouth ain't. One of these days it'll get you into trouble."

Spiteful words gathered on my tongue, but I'd baited the old man enough. I lifted my chin and gave him glare for glare.

Cecil turned from me to shout, "Edna, goddamn it, let's go!" He gunned the motor.

A quick look of understanding passed between Edna and Cleome before Edna hurried back to the truck. It was a stretch for her to get from the running board to the seat, but once she'd made the climb, Cecil released the clutch, and the truck spun gravel down the drive.

Cleome went to her husband's side. "Poor woman," she murmured.

"She should be used to Cecil's behavior," I commented. "They're the same age my mom would have been. In their seventies. Been married for years, and he hasn't changed."

Evan grinned, revealing the gap in his teeth. It gave him an impish look. "I think he's worse."

"Shame on you, Evan Miller," chided Cleome mildly. Looking at the casserole in her hands, she said, "I'll take this to Rosalie. She hasn't had any appetite. Maybe Edna's cooking will tempt her."

Evan surprised Cleome and me when he suggested, "Bretta might like to go, too." He added words in his Amish dialect. Her response was clearly negative, his filled with determination.

I felt like a third wheel, a turd in a punch bowl. No one had asked me if I'd like to make a condolence call, which I didn't. I had nothing to offer Rosalie but empty words of sympathy. A bouquet in hand had often eased me into a difficult situation, because the flowers worked as an icebreaker. Of course, in this case, flowers would be the last thing Rosalie would want to see.

While I'd been thinking, Cleome and Evan had come to an understanding. One look at Cleome's downturned mouth told me it hadn't been amicable. She marched off to Rosalie's. I reluctantly followed.

I fell into step next to her, cutting my stride in half to match hers. "I'm not here to cause trouble," I said.

"No need for you to be here at all."

"Evan asked me to come, to help him find out what happened. What do you think?"

"It's not for me to think," she said sharply. "We aren't put on this earth to question or to exact retribution. If someone harmed Isaac, it is written by our Lord, 'Vengeance belongeth unto me, I will recompense, saith the Lord.'"

"That might be fine for the hereafter, but what about now? Don't you think the person who harmed Isaac should be punished?"

"God deals out punishments. Job asked, 'Why do bad things happen to good people?' To this there is no answer. This is God's plan. He leads. We follow. It's wrong for any of us to interfere."

I was no match for this woman. I couldn't quote scripture. I couldn't substantiate any views I had with passages from the Bible. I kept quiet, and we arrived at Rosalie's in silence.

As we came up to the front, we heard voices from behind the house. All I could distinguish were male and female. Cleome heard something more. She cocked her head and listened. Without a word, she popped open the door, set the casserole on a table, then brushed past me.

I wanted to ask her what was going on, but I'd seen the steely glint in her eye. She didn't tell me not to, so I trailed her down the path that ran alongside the house to Isaac's cutting shed. I couldn't help wincing as I watched her bare feet stomp across the gravel. She seemed immune to the pain, her feet as tough as the soles on my shoes.

A battered green van was parked near the shed. It hadn't been there long. I could hear the ping of hot metal contracting as the motor cooled. I watched as a man, standing in front of the van, sucked on a cigarette, then ground it out under the heel of his boot.

He wore a cap pulled low over his eyes. His jeans were grimy. A rip in the knee had been mended by an inexperienced hand. He appeared to be in his fifties, overweight, with most of the flab centered around his middle. His belt rode under his belly and high on his back. The material of his dingy white T-shirt was stretched thin, and I could see the protrusion of his navel through the cloth.

Rosalie was facing him with her back braced against the shed door. She was like a lovely pregnant doll, her bone structure delicate, her eyes a soft doe brown. Twin spots of bright red blazed across her high cheekbones. When she saw us, a look of unmistakable relief crossed her pretty face.

"Mr. Hodges has come to offer me a deal," she said in a trembling voice.

"Deal?" snapped Cleome. "What kind of deal?"

Hodges likely wanted to ignore Cleome, but it's hard to overlook someone with as penetrating a gaze as hers. "Yes, ma'am," he said. "Isaac trusted me to truck his posies to River City. Now that he's . . . uh . . . gone, I'm offering to help his wife."

Cleome's eyebrows dipped low. "What do you know

about Isaac's work? You only hauled his flowers. You never helped grow or cut them."

Hodges puffed out his chest and reached into his pocket. He pulled out the flattened pack, extracted a cigarette, took his time lighting it. After he had the end glowing red, he said, "That's true, ma'am, but Isaac and me talked a lot. The way I see it, we'd do a sixty/forty split. Since I'll be doing all the work, I'd get the sixty end."

My eyes widened. The man had nerve but not much else. I wanted to say something, but I'd seen the deputy sidle closer. This conversation would be repeated to Sid. I figured if I kept my mouth shut and didn't call attention to myself, I'd be better off.

Hodges waved his hand airily. "Can't be that hard to grow a few posies. A little water here. A little horse sh—— manure there. And you've got yourself a profit."

Rosalie was shaking her head. "I don't think—"

Hodges didn't let her finish. "Look. You won't have to think. I'd do all of that and hand you a check. The way I see it, Isaac didn't charge enough. From what I've heard, those money-grubbing florists are ready to pay big bucks for Isaac's posies."

Stay in the background after a comment like that? No way. "Oh, they are?" I asked. "Where'd you hear that?"

Hodges hitched up his pants and swaggered closer. With his eyes on my chest, he stated, "I hear things. Ask questions. Talk to folks."

"Anyone in particular?"

34

He swallowed, then said, "I get around."

"I'll just bet you do," I muttered.

Hodges took his eyes off my chest long enough to give my jeans-clad figure a sharp appraisal. "Who the hell are you?" he demanded. "You ain't no Amish."

I rolled my eyes. "Duh. What was your first clue?"

Hodges scowled. "Back off. This don't concern you."

"But it does concern me," said a deep voice ringing with authority.

I jerked my head around and saw an Amish man standing by the rear bumper of the van. Behind me I heard a sharp intake of breath and glanced back as Cleome and Rosalie moved together and joined hands. Their eyes were downcast, their faces pale.

The Amish man had his back to the morning sun. The bright light concealed his face but outlined his tall, lank, stoop-shouldered frame. He moved closer. He was well past seventy, but age had favored him with strength and power in the lines of his face. A white beard rested on his chest. His skin was tanned from hours in the sun. His eyes, bright and strong, were illuminated with purpose. He didn't waste time letting us know what that purpose was.

After acknowledging Rosalie and Cleome with a brief nod, he ignored me and turned to Hodges. "We thank you for your visit, but we look after our own. Isaac's Rosalie will not want for anything."

In his Amish dialect he spoke softly to Cleome and Rosalie. They each nodded once and, without a word, walked to the house.

Hodges called, "Hey! Wait. We're not done yet. I want to know . . ." Their answer was to pick up their pace. By the time they got to the house, they were almost running.

Hodges spun on the old man. "Why'd you do that? What right do you have poking your nose in this private conversation?"

I didn't know this Amish man either, and at this point, I was interested, too.

He drew himself up to his full height. "I am Eli Detweiler, bishop of this district."

"Bishop?" scoffed Hodges. "That don't cut no butter with me. All my dealings were with Isaac. You never had any say before, and by damn, I don't see where you get off horning in now."

"As bishop, it's my job to look after everyone. Our lives are simple. We want for nothing. Isaac's flowers will die with him."

Once again, I couldn't stay quiet. "Die?" I said. "What do you mean, they'll die?" I thought perhaps he was speaking metaphorically. Apparently, this wasn't the case.

Detweiler looked at me, then he looked at Hodges. I didn't want the bishop to assume Hodges and I were together, so I quickly introduced myself.

"A florist?" he said. "I see. Then I'm sure you won't understand. Our children are a gift from God. This is the way we are to view flowers. They bring joy, peace, and reverence to our lives." His voice deepened. "But we *do not* profit by them. God has given us this bountiful land to raise grain to nourish our bodies, not grow flowers for sale."

Compared to this man, Hodges was a pesky gnat. "What will become of Isaac's hard work?" I asked, though I had a pretty good idea.

"The land will be returned to God."

Waste not . . . want not. Was that in the Bible? I was out of my depth here. Still, I couldn't let it go. "Isn't it wrong to just throw away all of Isaac's work?"

"We don't look to you for approval. The Lord sanctions our deeds, and misusing the soil is a sin."

I knew that as bishop, Detweiler didn't rule alone. "Was this the council's decision?"

He seemed surprised at my knowledge of their community. He pursed his lips and nodded once.

"When did you last have a conversation with Isaac?"

Detweiler's disapproval of me was growing. "That's not important."

When I visit with Evan, I try to curb my tongue because I value his friendship and I don't want to overstep any boundaries. With Detweiler, that wasn't the case. I felt uneasy about him. "Did you see Isaac the evening he died?"

Had we been alone, I'm not sure how Detweiler might have answered or if he'd have answered me at all. Hodges had been fidgeting like an impatient child waiting for his turn to speak. He picked that moment to butt in.

"Look," he grumbled, "I want to know if I'm out of a job."

"Yes," said Detweiler without hesitation.

"That decision hasn't been made," countered Evan as he came across the yard.

It would have taken a chain saw to cut all the tension in the air. Evan kept his eyes on the bishop but directed his words to Hodges.

"Leray, I'll have Isaac's crop ready for you to pick up at the usual time."

Detweiler had watched Evan's approach without comment. Not once did he contradict Evan's words. They faced each other, their faces immobile. Wordlessly, Detweiler turned. He detoured around Isaac's flower field, acknowledged the deputy with a brisk nod, and walked across the mowed pasture.

"Where's he going?" I asked Evan.

"He's taking a shortcut to his house over on the gravel road."

Hodges tipped back his cap and said, "That old codger is one mean son of a . . ." His words trailed off. He jerked his head in the direction Detweiler had taken. "You gonna let Isaac's posies die?"

I was sure Hodges didn't give a rat's ass about the flowers. All he was worried about was losing out on what he considered a profitable venture.

Evan sighed wearily. "I don't know."

"Well, if you ask me," began Hodges.

"He didn't." I'd had all I could stomach of this odious man. "He said he'd have the flowers ready for you. You got what you came for."

"Not really," said Hodges. "Like I was telling Isaac's widow, I think we should—"

"Now isn't the time," said Evan firmly. "The subject is closed."

Hodges wanted to argue, but Evan looked formidable. With a quirky salute, Hodges lumbered to the van. Once he had the engine going, he backed out, leaving a cloud of dust behind and a bad taste in my mouth.

"I don't trust that man," I said. I softened my tone as I added, "I'm not sure about Bishop Detweiler, either." When Evan didn't volunteer a comment, I asked, "Is he new to your community?"

Evan hesitated. For the first time, I got the feeling he might be sorry he'd called me. It was one thing for me to question my own people. It was another for me to question his.

Finally he answered, "Last fall, Eli was chosen to lead our community when Bishop Seth Fisher was called home to God. Seth's views were more liberal, and he accepted Isaac's plan to grow flowers." Evan rubbed a hand wearily across his face. "Bretta, our people don't make hasty decisions. Once a bishop is chosen, he's bishop for life, and his beliefs are carried from one district to another."

I turned and looked at Isaac's flowers. I sighed, trying to understand Detweiler's way of thinking. Wasn't any creative gift from God? Still looking at the flowers, I apologized. "I'm sorry, Evan, I just don't see the problem. Raising flowers seems so harmless. Who can it hurt?"

"Isaac," murmured Evan softly.

Were the flowers the motive for Isaac's murder? I turned around to ask him if that was what he meant. But Evan was striding toward the house, and it wasn't flowers on his mind.

A hearse had pulled into the driveway. Isaac was home. That was what Evan was talking about. My heart sank. The sheriff's car had pulled in, too.

Chapter Four

A somber scene unfolded as Evan received his brother's body. Margaret Jenkins slid from behind the steering wheel of the hearse. She's in her sixties, her hair gray. Judging from the thickness of the braids that wrapped her head like a coronet, it's very long. Her lantern jaw gave her face a gaunt, stern expression. Her eyes could be kind, her voice resolute and strong.

While I wouldn't classify Margaret as a close friend, we were well acquainted. It's always in a florist's best interest to be on good terms with the local funeral director.

I'd never been to an Amish funeral. I didn't plan to attend Isaac's. A few months ago, when I'd taken an after-hours delivery to the Woodgrove Funeral Chapel, Margaret and I'd gotten into a discussion about the Amish. She'd been free with her knowledge, and I'd sat longer than I'd planned, listening to her talk.

She had told me that she embalms the body and dresses it in a simple cotton shift, then delivers the deceased to his family. They dress him in clothes usually reserved for Sunday worship or other special occasions.

Today, Margaret acknowledged me with a conservative smile. She shook Evan's hand before she moved to the rear of the hearse and opened the door. A stout, take-charge woman, she grabbed hold of the stretcher and rolled it out. The wheels dropped into place with a clatter. The sheriff motioned for a deputy to take the lead. With Evan's help, they rolled Isaac across the yard. Cleome held the door open. .

Suddenly, Rosalie burst from the house and ran past Cleome. I was surprised to see Margaret, who remains dignified at any given moment, leave her end of the stretcher. On the uneven ground, the stretcher tipped. I heard Sid say, "What the hell?" as the men scrambled to keep the body in place. My attention moved to Margaret and Rosalie. They embraced with fondness.

Margaret put her lips close to Rosalie's ear. Whatever she said made the younger woman nod her head twice and wipe at her tears. I glanced at Cleome and saw her frowning at this open display of grief from Rosalie.

The men carried Isaac up the steps. Margaret, her arm wrapped firmly around Rosalie's thick waist, disappeared after them. Cleome closed the door.

I figured the sheriff would stay inside with Evan and the family for more questioning. Margaret would be coming out, since her part in Isaac's homecoming was finished. I waited impatiently. I wanted to ask her about Eli Detweiler before Sid made an appearance. I wanted to know who was on the council. I was caught off guard when Sid stepped outside and headed straight for me.

I licked my lips uneasily. It wouldn't do to show my

nervousness to Sid. My chin came up a notch. Good. Don't be on the defensive.

Sid is short, about the same height as my own five feet seven, with round features, light red hair, and freckles so thick on his pale skin they look like a fungus. At forty-six, he insists that he's a confirmed bachelor. After Carl died, Sid had called me a few times to ask how I was, but I'd always been left with the impression that his inquiry had come from his friendship with my husband, not because my well-being was on his mind. He could be charming or rude, depending upon his mood and the circumstances. I was loitering on the fringes of a murder scene, so I had a pretty good idea of my reception.

"Now, Sid, let's not—" I began, but he galloped past me toward the deputy who was guarding the field. I knew the drill when I saw the deputy consult a note-book. He pointed and gestured until he'd filled Sid's ears full.

Sid nodded once before backtracking to me. This time I didn't speak. I folded my arms across my chest and waited.

He stopped three feet from me and said, "My, my, you've had a lively morning, Bretta. Got your afternoon all planned out too, I suppose?"

"Paperwork is waiting for me at the flower shop."

"Good. Go do it."

He turned away, but my question stopped him. "How was Isaac murdered?"

Sid glanced at me over his shoulder and ground out, "Neck broke."

"Oh. Evan didn't tell—"

Sid spun on his heel and faced me. "Your Amish buddy isn't telling much of anything. I bet he also didn't tell you that he carried the victim to the house. That he scrubbed the goddamned body. That it was two hours before my office was notified."

I swallowed nervously. "What'll that do to your inquiry?"

"Don't you worry about *my* investigation. I'll do fine. Worry about why Evan Miller moved his dead brother from the scene of the crime. What was he trying to get rid of? What does he have to hide?"

"I'm sure Evan—"

"You're sure?" Sid barked a crude laugh. "I don't give a damn if you're sure or not. I'm the one who has to be satisfied."

I kept my voice even. "What I meant was, I don't think Evan was intentionally destroying evidence. He wouldn't think of the field as a crime scene."

Sid made a show of wiping a hand across his forehead. "Well, *that* relieves my mind."

I didn't like the way his mind was working. "You're being unreasonable, Sid."

"And you're keeping me from my job. Don't presume upon our friendship, Bretta." He rested his hands on his gun belt and threw back his shoulders. "Dealing with these people would try the patience of Job. It's up to me to find the truth." He stared at the house. Softly,

44

so I had to strain my ears, he murmured, "And nothing or nobody is going to keep me from it."

I was so caught up in my thoughts that when I left Evan's house, I turned the wrong way, taking the scenic route back to River City. This time I could have been riding through a trash heap for all the good the beauty did me.

I told myself I didn't for a minute believe Evan was responsible for Isaac's death. But why hadn't he told me up front about moving and washing the body? Was Sid right? Did Evan have something to hide? He hadn't told the sheriff about Katie seeing someone in the field with Isaac. I was in an awkward position. If I told Sid, I'd jeopardize Evan's confidence. If I didn't tell, I'd be screwing with a murder investigation.

I knew the Amish wanted others to respect their right to choose how they lived their lives. Like most of us, they don't want interference or persecution. But thinking of Eli Detweiler made me wonder if persecution was being practiced within their own Amish community.

Automatically, I took my foot off the accelerator as I approached the curve where the three boys had died in the car wreck. Somehow it didn't seem right to speed uncaringly past. I glanced at the spot, then stomped on the brakes.

In the time I'd been at Evan's, someone had placed a wreath at the side of the road. I recognized that oversized wreath. The last time I'd seen it, it had been hanging in my shop window, the focal point of my fall display. I'd made it myself. Bronze, orange, and gold silk chrysanthemums on a twenty-four-inch circle of grapevine. I'd tucked dried nuts, berries, and bittersweet among the colorful foliage. Pricey at one hundred and twenty-five dollars, I figured it wouldn't sell. Yet here it was, fastened to a wire easel that was pushed into the ground.

A car came up behind me, blared its horn, and swung around me. The driver glared as he passed. As if I needed another reminder this curve wasn't safe to park and gawk. I checked my mirror and pulled away.

I'd told Sid I had paperwork at the shop. Routine stuff, but the thought of seeing who'd spent over one hundred dollars on that wreath made me press harder on the accelerator.

Once I was in River City, I drove down Jefferson Street, turned left on Hawthorn, passed two law offices, an insurance agency, and would have breezed on by the Pick a Posie flower shop, except the owner, Allison Thorpe, was standing outside at her delivery van and saw me coming. She stepped to the edge of the street and flagged me down. Traffic is light on Saturday, since most of the surrounding businesses are closed. I pulled into a vacant slot.

Before I could get the lever into park, Allison pecked on my window. One look at her face told me she was on a mission. For an instant, I was tempted to lock my door and drive away. But I knew Allison. She'd hunt me down and have her say anyway.

Reluctantly, I pushed the button and lowered the window. "Hi, Allison. Working late?"

No polite "How are you?" from this woman. "Where've you been? I called your shop several times but was told you weren't in. I called your house and got that blasted answering machine."

I smothered a sigh. Allison—the name conjured up adjectives like dainty, wispy, tinkling. Instead, I faced bristly eyebrows that needed trimming with a hedge clipper. Deep-set eyes, a hawkish nose. An attitude that would make the pope throw up his hands in despair.

"I've been running errands," I said. "What did you want?"

She looked down her nose at me. "I'm calling a meeting of the area florists."

"Why?"

"A coalition is needed."

"Coalition?" I said. "What for?"

She thrust her jaw forward. "Isaac's flowers, Bretta. Get with the program. If we make the Millers an offer, we can hire someone to work the field and produce the flowers. We'll cut out Moth, the wholesaler, as the middleman. We'll all come out ahead."

I drummed my fingers on the steering wheel. My, my. It seemed that everyone had plans and deals for Isaac's flowers and the poor man was still above ground.

I dropped my gaze to the bouquet Allison held in her hands. Apparently, she'd been on her way to make a delivery when she'd spotted me. The florist in me perused the arrangement. Not bad. Good lines. Too sparse with the filler and greenery for my taste. The card read *Isabelle Quigley*. If those flowers were from her daughter, I was pissed. I usually got that order.

Allison was known for going to her competitors' customers and asking them outright to give her shop a chance. If they took her up on her offer, she'd add extra flowers the first few times. In the end, her parsimonious ways would take over. The customers became dissatisfied and went back to their original place of doing business.

The name of her shop, "Pick a Posie," was at the top of the envelope. Posie? You don't hear that word too often. Yet today I'd heard it several times.

A direct attack on Allison would net me nothing. On a whim, I decided to fish for information. I cast my line. "Who would we hire to work the field?"

Preening, she said, "As it happens I have someone in mind."

"Oh, really?" I jiggled the line. "We're talking quite an investment. Can we trust this person to do the work?"

She ignored the bait to look up and down the street. "This is poor business discussing something so important out here." She lowered her voice. "I've talked to the other four shop owners. They're interested."

"Busy, busy," I muttered.

"We have to jump on this. Measures have to be taken to preserve the quality of the flowers. They'll go downhill if left unattended."

I wasn't asking the right questions. I reeled in my

line and beefed up the lure. "I *might* be interested if I can be convinced we'll find someone suitable."

Allison beamed.

Not a pleasant sight. Allison pleased with herself is more annoying than Allison in a snit. "Before I decide anything, I'd want to interview this ... uh ... person."

She nearly wiggled with success.

I sank the hook, then watched her flounder as I laid out my conditions. "He'd have to be sharp, personable, have references. A college degree wouldn't hurt."

Allison struggled helplessly. "Well, now ... Bretta," she began slowly. Her words gathered speed as she tried to slip free. "Keep in mind we're dealing with a man of the soil. He's used to having dirty hands. We can't expect him to do the work in a three-piece suit."

I put my car in reverse. As I backed away, I landed her, left her gasping for air. "I don't imagine *Leray Hodges* owns a three-piece suit, Allison."

Her jaw went slack. She recovered enough to demand, "How did you—"

I cut her off in midsentence by squawking my tires on the pavement.

"Damned woman," I said aloud.

There were three fast-food restaurants in the ten blocks to my flower shop. In my present mood, I saw each of the three as pitfalls. I passed the first, my eyes straight ahead. Before I lost weight, I'd head immediately for food when my emotions got out of kilter. It didn't matter what I ate. Half a box of Hostess cupcakes—a bag of chips. At the second restaurant, I hesitated, even went so far as to reach for my turn signal. Still I drove on.

After my encounter with Allison, I felt that same old need to stuff my face. I told myself I was frustrated, irritated, and aggravated. I was *not* hungry. I guess I wasn't very convincing. At the third restaurant, I moved out of traffic and zoomed into line at the drive-through window.

I fumed as I waited for my turn to order. Leray and Allison. Who'd contacted whom? A strange alliance, at first glance, but self-serving to both. Bottom line, they wanted Isaac's flowers. Did Isaac's death prompt one to call the other with this deal? Or had something been afoot before Isaac died?

"Your order, please," said the scratchy voice over the intercom.

"A double cheese—" I stopped. I couldn't say it. My toes curled in my sneakers. "Nah," I said. "Make that a Diet Coke."

At the take-out window, I ignored the smells wafting out. I paid, accepted the Coke, and drove the remaining blocks to the shop. I should have been proud of my willpower. All I felt was deprived.

During business hours I park in the alley. Today I took a spot out front. The shop windows were dark, the CLOSED sign in place. Lois hadn't been too busy if she could lock up on time.

The name of my business was painted above the door: THE FLOWER SHOP. Not very original, but its simplicity suits me. If I had to answer the phone thirty times a day with something cutesy, I'd gag. I guess my inventive competitors were less prone to nausea. Besides Allison's Pick a Posie, there were Perfect Petals, Fragrant Flowers, Buds and Blooms, and my personal favorite, Whoopsie Daisy.

My shop is narrow but deep, the entry door squarely in the middle with a display window on each side. The window on the right had a Halloween theme. A witch rode her broom across a full amber moon made of Styrofoam and covered with shimmering satin. Polyester stuffing pulled into gossamer strands represented cobwebs. Huge black rubber spiders hid in corners, waiting patiently for their next victim.

I moved a few steps closer and activated a sensor. The biggest spider, about the size of my hand, sprang at the glass. Its jaws opened to expose a blood red mouth. From a hidden microphone came a spine-tingling scream. Thanks to Lois's husband, Noah, a technical genius, my windows always have something special. The kids love it. The adults remember, and I have more than my share of River City's floral business.

On my left was the fall display. I eyed it critically. Lois had replaced the big grapevine wreath with a smaller one. The balance was off, but it didn't look bad. Monday would be soon enough to make something else.

I slipped the key in the lock and pushed open the door. Like a soothing emollient, aromas rushed to greet me. Roses, cinnamon, eucalyptus. I breathed deeply and locked the door behind me. In the shadows, I closed my eyes. It had been a tough morning. I needed to regroup.

This little piece of real estate was more familiar than any room at home. I knew every nook and cranny. I sipped my Diet Coke. It's a sorry life I lead to receive this kind of pleasure from walking through the door. My work has always been important to me. But after Carl died, the shop became my mate, my lover, my best friend. I work hard, but I play with it, too. I can be as creative or innovative as the mood strikes. I can make changes without permission. I can buy, sell, set prices at my own discretion. In a nutshell, I can do as I damned well please. And that's the way I like it. That kind of freedom is worth a lot to me.

I left the lights off in the showroom but flipped the switch for the ones in my office and the workroom. All the floors had been swept and mopped. The trash had been carried out. The day's shipment of fresh flowers had arrived, and the front cooler was filled with Lois's arrangements. Her combination of colors and flowers sometimes shocks me, but she has customers who ask specifically for her, so I keep my opinions to myself.

I headed for my desk. Since the call for the wreath hadn't come in before I left yesterday, I assumed Lois had received it this morning. I pulled out the batch of invoices for Saturday and flipped through them. Zero. Hmm—cash?

"Nothing wrong with that," I murmured, scanning the cash receipts.

Second from the bottom, I found it. No name at the top. Today's date. The word "wreath" in the blank for description of merchandise. A sheet of wrinkled white paper had been stapled to the invoice. I turned it over and read:

Florist:
Please place the fall wreath that's in your **window** at the site where those three boys died. Enclosed you'll find money for the wreath and the delivery charge for the Woodgrove area. The remaining cash is for your time.

No signature. Typewritten. Lois had made a note at the bottom of the invoice:

Bretta:
When I unlocked the shop this morning, I found the envelope crammed under the door. I took the deposit to the bank, but I put the *two* one hundred–dollar bills from this order in the money bag. The envelope is on your desk.

The way this order was placed and where it went gave me the heebie-jeebies.

The hairs on my neck gave an answering tingle.

Chapter Five

The envelope was ordinary. No marks. No writing. Not even my shop's name typed across the front. I laid it aside, along with the invoice for the wreath and the letter. I wasn't sure what I had or if it was important.

Two hundred dollars was a lot more than the average person would spend on a wreath that would sit on a country road. My delivery fee to Woodgrove is eight dollars. Why all the secrecy in making the order? Why all the extra money?

I knew Lois would have stashed the zippered pouch in its usual hiding place. I went to the holding cooler and switched on the light. It was there in the left-hand corner, nestled behind a container of flowers.

As I reached for the pouch, I saw a few of Isaac's flowers. Thoughtfully, I ran a finger over the golden petals of a zinnia. Something niggled at me. Some impression I'd gotten looking at Isaac's field. Or was it something someone had said this morning? What was it? It was so damned frustrating. The more I tried to remember, the more other thoughts intruded.

I unzipped the pouch and took out the two hundred-dollar bills. Old bills; not those new ones that look like Monopoly money. On impulse, I sniffed them. Odd. I sniffed again. Very, very subtle.

With the refrigerated air circulating among the flowers, I could be mistaken. Holding the money by the corners, so my scent wouldn't be on them, I stepped into the workroom.

This time when I put the bills to my nose, I was sure I smelled something other than my own shop. I know its scent. I also know Lois's. She likes dramatic fragrances. This was sweet, light, and faintly musty. As if the bills had been tucked away near powder or sachet.

Was I reaching here? Maybe. But I didn't want to lose this scent. I looked around the workroom for something to put the money in. My eyes lighted on the corsage work center. On the shelf were plastic boutonniere bags. Carefully, I tucked the money in the bag, worked the trapped air out, and taped it shut.

At my desk, I picked up the letter and sniffed it. I thought it smelled like the money, but I couldn't be sure. To be on the safe side, I removed the staple from the invoice and stored the letter in another plastic bag.

I sat in my chair, proud that I'd preserved evidence. Then I scowled. Evidence of what? Was I being ridiculous? With Isaac's murder uppermost in my mind, was I looking for foul play around every curve?

"Curve of the road?" I mumbled, thinking of the three dead teenagers. Hmm. Had the driver been distracted? By what? The accident had been investigated by the Missouri Highway Patrol. Surely, if foul play were suspected, they'd be hot on the trail. I'd heard nothing, not even a whisper that the wreck was anything more than an accident. So why did I feel uneasy? The wreath. It came back to that wreath, and the way the order had been delivered.

I closed my eyes and heard Carl's voice in my ear. "Let it alone until you have more information." I opened my eyes and sighed. Good advice, but where was I supposed to look for this mysterious data? I waited, but this time Carl's voice was irritatingly silent.

The ice in my Coke had melted. An experimental sip told me I didn't want any more of it. Beads of moisture had run down the paper cup and left a ring on a trade magazine I'd planned to read. I reached for a tissue. As I wiped the glossy cover, I saw that my subscription was about out. Stamped on the front were the words: AN-NUAL SUBSCRIPTION HAS EXPIRED. TIME TO RENEW!

"Annual?" I murmured. "Annuals?"

My brain kicked in. That's what had been bothering me in the cooler. To make sure I was on the right track, I pulled a flower catalogue from a shelf. Next, I hunted up my last invoice from River City Wholesale Floral Company. Item by item, I went down the list, checking each type of flower against its description in the cata-logue:

Celosia—Yes

Cosmos—Yes

Zinnias—Yes

Except for the baby's breath, all the flowers in Isaac's

field were annuals. It was September. Missouri is usually hit with a killing frost in October. Once the night temperatures drop, the flowers die.

So why all the hoopla over Isaac's flowers? At the most there might be three more weeks of cutting time. Nature would take its course, the flowers would be gone, and Detweiler would get his way. Hodges wouldn't make that much money from three cuttings. Why was he so anxious to get control of the flowers? Or was it Allison who wanted control? Had she roped in Hodges? I shrugged. Regardless of who had contacted whom, the question was why. Why all this interest in a bunch of flowers that would be dead in a few weeks?

I rubbed my eyes wearily. My stomach rumbled, letting me know it was time to put something in it. Something healthy, not a double cheeseburger, though my mouth watered at the thought.

The invoice from River City Wholesale Floral Company lay on my desk. Noting the phone number under the letterhead, I impulsively dialed. It was a long shot that anyone would answer on a Saturday afternoon.

To my surprise, a man picked up the receiver and growled, "Damnit, Louise, I said I'd be home by four."

"Uh . . . is this River City Wholesale?" I asked.

Silence greeted my question. I pictured his indecision. He could either admit I had the right number and therefore have to deal with me, or he could say I'd misdialed.

I waited to see which way he'd go. Finally, he sighed.

"Yes, this is River City Wholesale, but we're closed. To-day *is* Saturday."

"I'm sorry to bother you. This is Bretta Solomon. I have the Flower Shop."

"Which shop?"

"The Flower Shop. Solomon. On Hawthorn."

"Oh, yeah. The big wom—good customer," he amended hastily. "This is Moth, but if you're calling about your statement, you'll have to wait until Monday when Cheryl's in her office."

"This isn't about my statement, Mr. Moth. I'd like to drive out and talk to you."

"About what?"

I should have thought this out more carefully. What did I want to talk to him about? Not Isaac's murder. Sid would cover that. Keep it simple. "Isaac Miller's flowers," I ventured.

"From what I understand, the flowers will be here at the usual time. Place your order, and we'll do the rest."

So Moth already knew the flowers would be delivered on schedule. Interesting. Leray Hodges was on the ball. He'd talked to Allison. He'd talked to Moth. What else had he been up to?

"This isn't about the delivery," I said. "I think it might be in your best interest if you'd talk to me. I won't take up too much of your time." I glanced at my watch. "I can be there in fifteen minutes."

"I don't know what this is about, but...all right. Come to the side door on the east. Go up the stairs. My office is at the end of the hall." He laughed lightly. "You can't miss it."

"Thank you," I said, and hung up before he could change his mind.

I switched off the lights, picked up the two plastic bags containing the money and the letter, and hurried out to my car. I didn't want to stuff the packets in my purse, so I locked them in the glove compartment.

My destination was across town on the outer fringes of the city. I'd given myself a deadline of fifteen minutes. I took a shortcut past the county courthouse, traveled down Truman Avenue, then hung a right on Duvall. This put me in the older section of town. Here the streets were narrow, some still paved with bricks. After several blocks, I made a left onto Carriage Road. Its claim to fame was as the historical starting point from where the rest of the town had taken shape. The street hugged the bluffs, and at one point I caught a glimpse of the river in the distance.

River City was founded in 1810 by a group of pioneers, lost in the vast Missouri wilderness, on their trek west. They'd come to the Osage River, had made camp to discuss their next move, then never left.

The group's leader, James Horton, has been credited with being blessed by divine guidance when he settled here. I had my own opinion. I'd seen a portrait of Horton's wife hanging in the River City Museum. Stern eyes, stubborn jaw, generous mouth. I figured Hattie Horton had grown tired of her husband's wanderlust. Unwilling to take another step, she'd dug in her heels and proclaimed this stretch of virgin Missouri soil home. I liked to think that Hattie was the original "liberated" woman. She'd stood up for her rights, pointed out that she was tired of weevils in her food, baths in a creek, and wheels under her butt. Now, years later, River City residents were profiting from her taking a stand.

With two minutes to spare, I pulled into the warehouse parking lot. At one time the two-story gray building had been a livestock auction barn and slaughterhouse. The holding pens were long gone, the cattle trailers replaced with a fleet of burgundy delivery vans. On the ground floor were the supply rooms where items of the floral trade were stocked. The room-size coolers that had once chilled freshly killed animals now held flowers.

As I got out of my car, I thought about J. W. Moth. I usually deal with a sales rep, or I do my ordering over the phone. I didn't know Moth personally, but I'd seen him presiding over the open house the company held twice a year—springtime and Christmas. He was a prissy little man, fastidious in his appearance. Every hair, what there was of it, always in place.

After crossing the parking lot, I rounded a corner of the building and found a door helpfully marked OFFICE. I tested the knob. It was unlocked as promised. I opened it and was confronted by a long, steep flight of dusty wooden stairs. I tilted my head back and saw another door at the top.

I heaved a sigh and started the climb. By the time I reached the last step, my feet were dragging, my breath coming in painful gasps.

"Gotta get more exercise," I wheezed. When I could breathe normally, I swung open the door. "We spare no expense" was the cynical thought that ran through my brain.

The corridor was dingy, illuminated by three bare bulbs, their wattage more in keeping with a spook show than a place of business. To my right was an alcove with two vending machines. A trail of round blotches on the beige carpet gave evidence of sloppy practices. I followed the path and saw that the spots ended at the door to billing. I vowed to look over my statement with a more critical eye if this was any indication of the people who manned the computers.

All but one door was closed, the rooms dark behind frosted glass. From the one open door, sunshine pooled in the hall, and I hurried toward it.

I paused to let my eyes adjust to the light, then raised my hand to knock. I froze before I could connect with the door frame. Pecan paneling, aqua carpeting, and an outside wall made of glass were the grandiose setting of a room that was a "road kill" museum.

Two squirrels were staged on a tree branch that was suspended from the ceiling. A skunk peeked at me from behind a woven basket. Deer heads were mounted on the walls. An opossum was frozen in time, his glassy eyes stretched wide, as if amazed at his predicament.

Moth stood smiling behind his desk. His face was

thin, his eyes dark and direct. Narrow lips and a pointed chin did nothing for his physical appearance.

"Mrs. Solomon?" he squeaked in a high-pitched voice. "I haven't seen you for a while." His eyes grazed my face, then meandered in a long, lazy stroll down the length of my body. "You've changed," he said softly. "Very nice. Very nice indeed."

Did he think I'd be interested in him? Only when these animals could twitch their tails.

When I continued to stand in the doorway, Moth gave me a smile that made his lips disappear. "Won't you come in?" he invited.

I nodded politely. I perched on the chair he offered and forced myself to sit quietly and not crane my neck. It wasn't until Moth took a seat that I saw the snake. It lay in a glass case on the corner of his desk. As big around as a kindergartner's pencil, the creature looked to be two feet long. Its color was the same shade of Nile green as the apples I'd been forbidden to eat as a child. The snake moved, and I felt the same queasiness I'd had then when I'd snitched too many apples.

Moth followed my gaze. "I see you've spotted Harvey." He plucked off the lid and stuck his hand in the case.

I was close enough to see the snake's tongue flicker. He apparently liked what he smelled because he glided up Moth's arm and circled it like a bracelet. "I taught him to do that," bragged Moth.

I gestured to the room's other occupants. "Doesn't their fate make him a little nervous?"

Moth ignored my question and thrust his arm out to me. "You want to hold him?"

I managed to quell a shudder. "Not this time. Maybe later."

Moth nodded, not surprised. He eased the green lasso off his arm and dropped it back into the case. Instead of putting the lid in place, he picked up a sheaf of papers. "Let's get on with this. I want to look over these notes and still have time to change into my tuxedo." In a smug voice, he explained, "I'm master of ceremonies at tonight's taxidermy gala."

Taxidermy gala? Not two words I'd think of in the same sentence. I was glad my flower shop hadn't gotten that order. What would I have used for centerpieces? I pictured blue delphiniums and red roses artistically arranged around a preserved raccoon. I turned off my lurid imagination and smiled pleasantly. "I'll try not to keep you."

"Yes, well. Why did you want to see me?"

It took me a second to rethink my reasons for being here. Harvey wasn't helping, slithering around his case. I cleared my throat and took my gaze off the snake. Looking at Moth wasn't much better. His eyes gleamed at me. "Did you know Isaac Miller was murdered?" I blurted. So much for leaving this in Sid's hands. I watched Moth for his reaction. I'd hoped for open-mouthed disbelief. What I got was mild surprise. I guess a man who has a snake for a pet isn't caught off guard easily.

Moth raised his eyebrows. "Really? Of course, I heard

there's to be an autopsy. But murder?" He clicked his tongue distastefully.

"How much longer will Isaac's flowers be available?"

Moth grimaced. "How should I know? Depends on the weather. Middle to the end of October."

"Did Isaac mention that he might have to stop growing them?"

He leaned back in his chair and tossed the papers on his desk. "*He* didn't."

I caught the emphasis and asked, "Did someone else tell you?"

"Yes, but I don't take much stock in someone who calls and doesn't have the decency to identify himself. I ignored the call."

"Was it a man or a woman?"

"It could have been either. We didn't have a lengthy conversation. The person told me to stop buying flowers from the Amish man. He hung up. So did I."

"Did you mention this to Isaac?"

"Sure. Why not?"

"No reason. How did he react when you told him?"

"I don't know. Surprised." Moth rethought his answer. "No, not surprised, more like resigned. I really don't remember."

"When was this?" I asked.

Moth shifted restlessly in his chair. "A few weeks ago."

"Did you know there's a plan among some of the florists to cut you out as middleman?"

His pointed chin shot up. His eyes closed to slits. "Where'd you hear that?"

I took a page from Hodges's prolific repertoire of words. "I see people. Talk. Get around."

Abruptly, Moth stood up. "This is a waste of my time. I don't know what you're up to, but if it's to cause trouble, you've come to the wrong man. Isaac and I had an agreement. No one"—his voice deepened dramatically—"and I mean no one but me will be able to buy anything Isaac Miller had a hand in growing." He came around the desk. "If that's all, Mrs. Solomon," he said, "I have to get home and change."

Slowly, I walked to the door. "With Isaac's death, won't your agreement become invalid?"

"No, it will not. I have the situation well in hand."

In the doorway, I turned with another question. Before I could ask it, Moth exclaimed, "Get back in here, you little rascal."

I knew he wasn't talking to me. Harvey must have made his escape. I did the same. I hurried down the corridor, past the vending machines, down the staircase. I didn't take a full breath till I was sitting in my car.

Chapter Six

I carried the stepladder out of my garage and set it by the front steps. With my hands on my hips, I gazed above me. There it was, my newspaper, teetering on the edge of the gutter.

With each step up the ladder, I swore I'd get to the bottom of these shenanigans. What had I done to this kid? I racked my brain but couldn't come up with a single thing. At first, I'd figured the boy was going through puberty, and his mind was on something else. But after talking to a couple of neighbors, I discovered that the placement of my paper was a calculated prank. None of them were experiencing this kind of treatment.

I tucked the paper under my arm and put the ladder away. I didn't know the kid. He'd been on the route for about six months. I had a telephone number and a name: Jamie Fenton. I'd seen him only once, about a month ago. I'd come home early from the shop with a sick headache. When I heard the thud of the paper hit the side of the house, I'd gone to the front door. He was too far down the street to call to, but I'd seen a pudgy kid, a ball cap, and chubby legs pedaling for all they were worth.

A confrontation was in order. I could complain to the newspaper office, but I wanted to look this kid in the eye.

Shaking my head, I sat down at the kitchen table, unfolded the paper, and picked up my fork. Eating and reading at the same time is a diet no-no. With a limited amount of food, I'm supposed to savor each bite. Delight in the texture; thrill to the taste. In short, get as much out of the food as I possibly can. A tough assignment when faced with a can of tuna dumped on a bed of shredded lettuce. I might have been more creative, but I wasn't in the mood. Glancing down at the front page, today's headline finished the job on my spiritless meal:

AMISH MAN MURDERED IN FLOWER FIELD

I pushed my plate aside and gave full attention to the story. My frustration grew as I read to the end. Nothing I didn't already know.

My conversation with Moth had left too many questions unanswered. I took a notebook from a drawer and made a list. When I was finished, I nudged my plate closer and took a bite of tuna. I studied the paper and saw a few loose ends could be tied up, if I could phone Evan. Since that was impossible, I tried another route.

Allison's home number isn't on my frequent caller list. I looked it up, and after taking a deep breath, I dialed. While it rang, I muttered, "I must be desperate."

"Hello," she trilled.

"This is Bretta."

A moment of stunned silence, then Allison regained her equilibrium. "Tough luck, Bretta. You're out. We're in." She hung up.

"In what?" I said, slamming down the phone. "Deep shit, if you ask me." Which she had, and I'd turned her down.

Hindsight. I should have played her, let her have plenty of line. If she thought I was on her side, I'd have information. As it was, all I had were conflicting statements. How could Allison be in if Moth had an agreement with Isaac? Allison had said the coalition would cut Moth out and have more profit. It couldn't work both ways.

Quickly, I gave my fingers more exercise. I found another competitor's home number. As soon as I identified myself, she hung up. Three more times I made calls to area florists. Each time I was rebuffed, politely but firmly.

Allison had done her work well. She'd sewed up the coalition with a steel thread. I was shut out. No information, not a clue as to their plans. Hadn't it occurred to any of them that Isaac's flowers were annuals? That they might be putting together a package deal that was going nowhere? I tapped my fork against my plate until the racket I was making annoyed me. I was at a dead end.

There's a thought. "Dead?" I did another search in the phone book. I found the number and dialed.

In a deep, somber tone, Margaret answered, "Wood-grove Funeral Chapel."

"Margaret, this is Bretta Solomon. Got a minute?"

"Sorry, Bretta," she whispered. "A family is here making arrangements. We'll have to talk another—"

"Wait!" I interjected, in case she was going to hang up. I was getting a complex. Besides, there wasn't anyone else to call. "Can I see you? Tonight?"

"Tonight?" echoed Margaret in surprise. "No, I—"

"Tomorrow, then? In the morning, unless you'll be in church."

Margaret sighed. "If it's important, tomorrow morning will have to do. Ten. I can't get away for church. I . . . uh . . . there are things to do here. Now if you'll excuse me, I have to say good-bye."

This time when I hung up, I was satisfied. I'd gotten something. I'd even gotten a kind farewell.

Sunday morning dawned bright and cool. I left the River City limits with a pair of sunglasses perched on my nose. I'd spent a lousy night. Saturday's events had played over and over in my mind without any results, except my eyes were heavy and my head throbbed. Three cups of coffee hadn't done any good. It was early, at least for me, on a Sunday. Just past eight-thirty. I hoped a leisurely drive to Woodgrove with the car window down would blow the dust off my brain.

Once again, I passed the turnoff to Woodgrove. I wasn't as interested in the scenery as I was in seeing if the wreath was still there.

When I came to the curve in the road, my heart jumped. At first, I thought there'd been another accident. I counted four cars parked along the side of the road. As I slowed, I saw a group of teenagers standing among the sheared-off trees and brush.

I didn't want to intrude on their grief, but this was too good a chance to pass up. I parked my car at the head of the line, left my sunglasses on the dashboard, and climbed out. The young people turned at my approach. There were fifteen in all. I saw tears. Red eyes. Several yellow roses. And the wreath.

Two boys were tying a black ribbon around the massive tree trunk, hiding the nasty gash. In silence, we watched them climb up the deep ravine, their sneakers slipping on the dewy grass as they clutched at mangled saplings to haul themselves to the top.

I waited until they were with the others before I spoke. "I'm sorry about your loss." I pointed to the wreath. "I own the flower shop where that was purchased."

"Who's it from?" asked a girl with long hair. "It doesn't have a card."

"That's why I stopped." Briefly, I explained about the note under the shop door.

A tall boy, older than the others, stepped forward. "I'm Josh Baxter. Ned was my little brother." Tears clogged his throat, making his words quavery. "He was behind the wheel. I taught him how to drive." His voice broke. "I thought I taught him well."

A couple of the kids touched Josh's arm. He nodded, took a deep breath, and pointed around the group. "That's Mike's brother, Steve. That's Eric's girlfriend, Heather. The rest are friends. Classmates of the guys."

"What do you think?" I asked softly. "Who do you think might have sent the wreath?" I studied their young faces. All shook their heads. Grief had left them vulnerable. Not one, but three important people had been taken savagely from their lives. I knew how death worked. This group would never be the same. It was sad. It was also damned unfair.

"Perhaps your parents sent it?" I offered.

Steve answered, "Never happened. The house reeks of flowers. Mom says she doesn't want to see another one ever again."

Josh said, "If my parents wanted something like this, they'd have discussed it with me."

Heads waggled agreement. I gave Josh one of my flower shop cards and asked, "If you should hear anything, would you get in touch with me?"

As I drove away, I looked in the rearview mirror. The group was huddled in a circle, their arms wrapped around each other's waists. For some people, this is the best way to deal with grief. To share it; to take solace in being with others who understand. It was a heart-wrenching scene. My throat tightened.

When Carl died, I'd suffered alone. Dad had sent a sympathy card. Carl's mother and brother live in Nashville. Irene is blind and lives in a nursing home; the trip to Missouri would have been too difficult for her to make. Darold, Carl's brother, was too stingy to fork out the cash for the trip.

There were friends, but nothing like this. I was touched by the depth of compassion in these young people. I envied their close relationship. It took a couple of tries before I could swallow the lump in my throat.

After Carl's death, I'd been numb. It had been months before the full realization of my loss had sunk in. Hard work and long hours helped, but often my lack of a family still seems overwhelming. I miss having someone to love. I'd give ten years of my life if I could pick up Carl's dirty clothes a few more times.

My destination didn't help my frame of mind. Woodgrove Funeral Chapel was two blocks off the main drag in a residential area. I parked on the street. Since I was early, I took my time walking to the front door.

The funeral home looked like the other houses on the block, except for the discreet sign posted near the driveway. In this part of the country, nearly all the funeral homes were initially family dwellings. Most are rambling two-story structures, with plenty of room on the ground floor for seating guests attending a service.

Margaret had an apartment upstairs, but not a separate outside entrance. I wondered what it would be like to live above a funeral home. Did she ever have guests over? Did she have to watch what she cooked, so the aroma of bacon or cabbage wouldn't linger in the slumber room?

I tried the door. It was locked. I walked around to

the side door, where flowers were delivered. It, too, was locked. I cupped my hands to the glass and peeked in. Dark. With time to kill, I decided to take a stroll to the rear of the property.

The day was as good as it gets in September—warm, a few clouds, and a breeze that was better than any mood-altering drug. The grounds were in tiptop shape. The hedges were neatly trimmed, the grass freshly mowed. Red geraniums in mammoth terra-cotta pots provided cheerful but tasteful dots of color.

A vegetable garden was well tended, the rows straight and weed-free. I recognized cucumber, squash, pumpkin, and okra plants. There were other rows, but I ignored them when I spied a ripe tomato gleaming like a ruby sitting on green velvet. I picked it, polished it on my sleeve, and took a bite. The succulent juices ran down my chin. Absently, I wiped them away and looked over the rest of the property.

The lot wasn't deep. There were no outbuildings. The garage was located under the house. The cement drive sloped down to two big doors. I checked the small windows. Only the black hearse. Margaret's car was gone.

Had she changed her mind about attending church? Had she forgotten I was coming?

I finished my snack and tossed the stem in a trash bin near the garage. I was feeling a bit miffed when the sharp toot of a horn called my attention to the street. I looked down the drive and saw Margaret arrive in a dusty black Cadillac.

She had the car door open before she'd turned off the engine. "Am I late?" she called.

"I'm early," I admitted.

She shut off the car, picked up her purse, and climbed out. I'd never seen Margaret in anything but a navy dress. Sometimes she pinned a brooch at her shoulder, but most of the time she was unadorned. Today, she was dressed in ratty black slacks, a black pullover, and soiled white tennis shoes. Her hair straggled from its customary neat style. The cuffs of her pants had collected hordes of tiny burrs.

She gave a self-conscious laugh. "Excuse how I look," she said. "I couldn't sleep and didn't feel like working, so I went scavenging."

What did an undertaker scavenge?

Margaret accurately read the question on my face and said, "Come. See for yourself." She went to the trunk of her car and popped up the lid.

I was more than curious. I peeked in and chuckled. Inside were three small pumpkins, some oddly shaped gourds, and a basket of assorted weeds. Their shapes, textures, and intense colors would make an aesthetic bouquet.

"How about giving me a hand?" she asked.

I nodded and picked up the pumpkins. Margaret grabbed the rest of the load, and we headed for the door. She continued a rapid-fire conversation. I didn't mind. I'd come to hear her talk. Later I'd steer the topic around to Isaac and the council. Until then, I was content to listen.

". . . something special in the front lobby. Once a funeral is over, and the flowers are gone, it seems kind of dreary." She juggled her burden, so she could fit the key in the lock. "Nothing quite so dominating as a Christmas tree or jack-o'-lanterns, but something that will soothe the families and friends when they come by to pay their respects."

"I'm surprised. Most funeral directors get their fill of flowers."

Margaret grunted success with the lock and pushed the door open. We stepped into the dark. On familiar ground, she rushed ahead. I followed more carefully. There were windows, but in this part of the chapel, they were covered with heavy draperies.

"I love flowers," said Margaret, her voice floating back to me in the dusky light. "My mother always had a garden. We had fresh-picked flowers on the table all summer. In the winter, when the flowers were gone, she'd use cut branches of cedar to give the house a special aroma."

She flipped on the office light, then sighed. "All these years later, I can't smell cedar without thinking of home."

I stood in the hall with the pumpkins. She stirred herself and apologized. "Here I am going on and on, and those pumpkins are cumbersome." She motioned with her chin to the far side of the room. "We'll put them in that closet. I'll arrange them later." She hurried around her desk and wrestled the door open. We set everything on the floor.

With her arms unburdened, Margaret gestured self-consciously to her clothes. "If you can stand to look at me, I'll wait to shower and change after you leave. In the meantime, I need a cup of coffee. Would you care for one?"

"I'd love it," I said. "I didn't sleep well, either."

Margaret stepped into a small room off her office. I followed and saw a kitchenette. I stood in the doorway and watched as she filled a percolator with water. I like my coffee strong, but I raised my eyebrows at the double measure she used.

While she took cups down from a cabinet, I found myself telling her about my trip to Moth's office and his decor. Her tongue clicked a few times—"tsk, tsk"—when I described the stuffed animals and Harvey, the snake. She frowned when I mentioned questioning Moth about Isaac's murder.

"Why are you getting involved?" she asked, leading the way back to her office. She nodded to a chair beside her desk.

I sat down and sighed. "I'm not sure. Evan wanted me to see why an autopsy was conducted when Isaac died. But the sheriff has answered that question." I sighed again. "I can't get Isaac's death out of my mind."

"Didn't your husband just pass away?"

"A little over a year ago."

"Sounds to me like you're lonesome. You have too much time on your hands."

Pop psychology from a funeral director. Humph. Instead of analyzing me, she could take a look at her own life. I knew her story. She'd been trained as a nurse but had traded occupations when her husband, Leon, was diagnosed with cancer. Before he'd become too ill to work, she'd gone to mortuary school. Once licensed, she'd taken over the funeral home when he passed away. In other words, she'd switched from saving lives to preserving death. Surely that deserved a couple of visits to a therapist.

"The flower shop keeps me busy," I said, "but I miss helping Carl with his investigations."

"You helped him? How?"

"Mostly, I listened. I was his sounding board. He'd tell me what was going on, who the suspects were, and I'd ask questions, poke holes in his theories. I liked it."

"But he was a trained policeman, my dear. You're"— she softened her words with a smile—"merely a florist."

I shrugged. "Mysteries fascinate me. However, it isn't just Isaac's death. The Amish are intriguing. I could never live like they do, and I'm not talking about the lack of phones, electricity, or automobiles. I'm too verbal. I'm always ready to question everything. To have one man tell me how to live would be frustrating."

"You're thinking of Bishop Detweiler?" When I nodded, she said, "He isn't telling them how to live, Bretta."

"It sounds like it."

"He's only telling his people how the Bible says they should live. Those aren't his rules. He doesn't make them."

"But he enforces them to his liking."

Margaret's tone was patient. "The Amish consider

themselves servants of God. He put them here on earth for a purpose and that purpose is written in the Bible."

"But if five different people read the same scripture," I argued, "there might be five different interpretations. Who decides what's right?"

Margaret frowned. "They have to believe that the man they've chosen is strong of character and will lead them down the right path."

"What of Isaac's flowers?" I asked. "Do you understand why Detweiler wants them to die?"

"Yes."

"Then would you explain it to me?"

"Grain is grown to feed their bodies, to keep them healthy, so they can worship the Lord. It's a sin to waste so much land on frivolous flowers. A few is a pleasure. Too many is an extravagance. Too worldly for the Amish."

I wasn't convinced, and it showed. Margaret waved a hand dismissively. "Bretta, Isaac is dead. To keep rehashing it will only bring hurt. If Evan lets the flowers die, then things can get back to normal."

"Normal?" I exclaimed. "How can they ever be normal? Isaac is dead. Rosalie is a widow. Her children will grow up without their father. What's normal about that?"

Margaret winced. "True," she murmured. Abruptly, she got to her feet and went to the kitchenette. "You're too outspoken for your own good," she called through the doorway.

"I've been told that before," I admitted. "I've also been called a Missouri mule."

She came back into the office carrying two steaming cups. Carefully, I accepted one and took an experimental sip. I tried not to make a face. This brew would grow hair on one of Margaret's pumpkins.

I set the cup down and mused aloud, "I can't help but think that Isaac was killed by someone he knew."

The cup of coffee in Margaret's hand tipped. Hot liquid spilled across the desk. Her knees buckled, and she flopped weakly into her chair.

Chapter Seven

I rushed around the desk, plucked a magazine off a shelf, and fanned Margaret. "Are you all right?" I asked.

She rubbed a trembling hand across her face. "I'm fine," she murmured. "I felt dizzy for a moment." She gave me a sheepish grin. "I've been trying to do too much. I forget I'm not as young as I used to be. The brain's willing to do the tasks, but the body's beginning to rebel."

I stopped fanning and stepped back. "Oh. I hoped maybe something I said jogged your memory, and you had a clue as to who'd killed Isaac."

Two rosy spots of color bloomed on Margaret's pale cheeks. She gave me a curt look before grabbing a handful of Kleenex from a box. As she blotted the soggy papers on her desk, she said, "The idea. Isaac knowing his killer. You grew up here, Bretta. You know these people just as well as I do."

"Someone killed Isaac."

"Leave that to the sheriff."

"But Evan asked me—"

Margaret's exasperated sigh cut me off. "Cecil said you were annoying, but I stood up for you." She tossed the brown-stained tissues in the trash. "Perhaps I was hasty in coming to your defense."

Cecil is the one who's a pain in the butt, but I didn't say that. I'd taken a good look at the magazine in my hand. No glossy pages. The words inside looked like gibberish. It was a much more interesting topic than Cecil's opinion of me, which was nothing new. I held the magazine up. "What's this?"

"It's a magazine."

"I know that. What kind? It's in a foreign language."

"Not foreign. It's an Amish publication called *The Budget*." She took it out of my hands and put it back on the shelf.

"And you subscribe to it?"

"Yes," she said wearily. "This town and these people are important to me. I can't afford to make a blunder when I deal with the Amish." Her tone turned waspish as she demanded, "Are you going to investigate that?"

What had started out as a congenial conversation was deteriorating. It was time to do some serious groveling.

"I'm sorry," I said. "I came to you because you understand the Amish. Apparently, you even speak their language. I admire you. So does everyone here in Woodgrove. You see people when their emotions are raw with grief. You give them comfort, make their burdens easier to bear."

Her chin quivered. "I try."

"I came to ask you who's on the Amish council. Did

they have the power to make Isaac stop growing his flowers?"

"Yes."

"Who are they?"

She hesitated, then answered, "There are three men. Eli Detweiler. Reuben Hosteiler. He moved to Woodgrove two or three years ago. Last fall, he lost a leg when his buggy had an accident with a car. Leo Mast is the third. He and his family have been visiting back east for the last few weeks. They're thinking of moving back to Pennsylvania." She bustled up from her desk. "Now, if you'll excuse me, I have work to do."

"One more thing." I kept talking, though the look on her face didn't invite me to continue. "How far would the discord between Isaac and Detweiler have gone?"

"What's too far?"

"Murder."

Margaret's mouth grew round with disbelief. She gulped twice before she could find her voice. "Are you accusing one of the Amish of murder?"

"I'm not accusing anyone. I'm merely looking at motive. Who would have a reason to kill a peace-loving man who grows flowers?"

"Why couldn't it have been a stranger? A vagrant?"

I raised my eyebrows in amazement. "Do you seriously believe that Isaac was murdered by someone passing by? Again, why? What's the motive?"

"I don't want to think about it," replied Margaret, "and you shouldn't—"

The phone rang. She turned her back on me and took

82

two deep breaths to compose herself. She picked up the receiver.

"Woodgrove Funeral Chapel," she said in a calm, precise voice.

She sounded normal, but when she smoothed her hair, I saw her hand tremble. I listened, not so much to the conversation as to the texture of her voice. Gentle, tranquil, resonant. A minute ago, she'd been upset with me. Now she was calm and helpful. She was good at her job. Very kind and patient with the people.

". . . funeral set for one o'clock Thursday here at the chapel. Yes. Yes. Visitation is Wednesday from seven till eight o'clock. That's true. The family is waiting for a daughter to fly in from Alaska. Something about a mixup with her tickets."

When she hung up, I asked, "What do you know about Bishop Detweiler?"

It was interesting to watch the varied emotions flash across her face. Margaret had been in her helpful mode when she replaced the receiver. At my question, her face did a reversal, searching for an appropriate hostile emotion. She settled on icy silence and marched out of the office. I stayed where I was and listened to her progress. Her gait was quick and solid. The woman was annoyed, but I wasn't going to be diverted.

I stepped into the hall. I'd never had a fear of the dark, death, or in this case, funeral homes. Carl had always said that events, situations, and places were merely the settings for violence. It's human beings who create the mayhem.

Margaret had disappeared, but she had switched on several lights. I gazed around me. The architecture of the old house was beautiful. Filigreed oak cornices decorated the ivory walls. A broad staircase rose six steps, then disappeared into a gracious curve to the second floor. The wood gleamed in the soft lighting. The house's present-day use made it difficult to see how it might originally have been arranged. Walls had been removed; others had been built. An eight-foot-wide corridor ran from the front door to the back.

Across from me was a cozy little room where family members could sit and reflect. Like the rest of the chapel, its carpet was hunter green. Mauve and burgundy—striped material covered padded chairs.

Next to the sitting area was a medium-sized slumber room. I could have been standing in someone's home. A couple of sofas, a coffee table with flower arrangement, two end tables, and several boxes of Kleenex. The focal point wasn't a television but a steel blue casket open at the top.

I stepped to the door and read the name on the register: MYRTLE RANKIN. I didn't think I knew her, but I checked to make sure. Nope. She'd been very old and extremely small. Her cheeks were bright with rouge, her lips a pale pink. There were two potted plants sitting on stands nearby. Across the casket's bottom lid was an example of Allison's economy casketpieces. I knew without counting it would have eighteen pink carnations and two bunches of leather leaf greenery among the sprigs of fern. Since ribbon is cheaper than flowers, the top of the spray was a mass of loops.

I turned away. The main chapel was farther down the hall. It held several rows of folding chairs but no casket or flowers.

Once I passed this slumber room, I was in unfamiliar territory. Carl's arrangements had been handled by a River City funeral home. When Mom had died, Leon was still director. This part had been added after his death.

A slice of light showed around the edge of a door. I hesitated. In an unfamiliar funeral home, you don't brazenly burst into a room unless you're prepared—for anything. I eased the door open, then pushed it wider when I saw all the empty caskets.

In my mind, it was the showroom, but I'd been informed by a funeral director friend that certain terms should always be used. It's cemeteries, never graveyards. Casket, never coffin. Funeral director, never undertaker. Remains or deceased, but never corpse. And this was a selection room, not a showroom.

I saw approximately twelve caskets in assorted colors and styles ranging from cheap to ornate. The lighting was bright, almost cheerful, if a room filled with caskets could be described as such. Brass and silver fittings gleamed.

Margaret was at the far end. She glanced up when I came in. "I'm sorry I snapped at you," she said. "I'm so upset. Poor Rosalie. One child, and another on the way."

"I know." I worked my way to her, dodging caskets of all kinds. Teal, mauve, walnut. Mahogany, gray, oak. Purple.

Purple? I stopped to trail a finger down the lavender satin lining. "This is different."

Margaret stopped tugging on a bronze metal casket. "I'm sending it back," she said. "I've had it since January. No one wants purple."

"I like it," I said, as I moved down the room toward her. "If it had one of *my* casketpieces of pink roses, a few purple asters to pick up the color, and some baby's breath, it would be striking."

"Yeah, well, striking doesn't sell in my business." She pointed to the casket she was trying to move. "No one is inventive. Families always pick this model for a man. Next time I get a delivery, I'm going to put it closer to the embalming room. I'm getting too old to roll it around."

I was ready to offer my assistance but got sidetracked when I saw an L-shaped metal handle lying on the cushy lining. I picked it up and asked, "What's this?"

"Some of the metal caskets have airtight seals that serve as a moisture barrier. That crank locks the seal in place."

I put the metal handle back where I'd found it. I took hold of the end of the casket she was struggling with and swung it away from the wall. "I'll help. Just tell me where we're going."

"Over there," she said, jerking her head to the left.

We maneuvered the casket across the carpeted floor and stopped before a pair of double doors. Margaret turned to me and asked, "Are you squeamish?"

I didn't answer right away. I was in a funeral home. I could move caskets. I could put a single rose in the deceased's hand. I could pin on a corsage if the family requested it. I gave an uneasy chuckle. "Depends on what you have in mind."

"I need to move Mr. Engelhart from the embalming table to his new home." She indicated the casket. "The hoist is getting worn and often lets me down"—she grimaced—"or I should say, let's *my guest* down too quickly." She waited a moment, then asked, "Will you help me?"

I looked at the doors. "Is he dressed?"

Margaret snorted. "He is now. I have yet to bury a naked body, though Priscilla Yarrowby came close. Flimsy little nightie. Black and red garter belt. I think I've seen it all, then something new crops up, and I'm taken by surprise all over again."

"How do you usually move the bodies?"

"Not bodies," she corrected. "The deceased. I prefer to call them 'my guest' or by name. My neighbor comes in to drive the family car and do odd jobs, but he's gone for the day."

Talk about odd jobs. But I smiled congenially. "You'll have to introduce me to Mr. Engelhart. I can't man-handle him without a proper introduction."

Margaret pursed her lips in light rebuke at my humor. She opened the doors to a world I'd only speculated on. While she positioned the casket, she took me at my word and began a long spiel on the life of Mr. Clarence Engelhart. While she talked, I gazed around the embalming room.

Green-tiled walls and floor. No windows. A porcelain table. Mr. Engelhart. My eyes skimmed over him. Glass-front cabinets on two walls. A drain in the floor. I swallowed. The area was about twelve by fourteen feet. We didn't have much room to move between the casket and the table. When this house had been a family dwelling, this might have been a small bedroom or a storage room. A pulley hung above the table. Its track looped across the ceiling to the doors where I stood.

". . . his death reminded me of Leon's. Long and painful," Margaret was saying.

I assumed she was talking about Mr. Engelhart. I nodded sympathetically, then asked, "Where do you want me?"

"The casket stays here. We bring Mr. Engelhart to it. The hoist works at one height, which is about a foot lower than I need. When I get him to the casket, I want you to help me raise him that twelve inches. If I get the hoist too high, it slips a cog and will drop the load."

"I've slipped a cog, too," I muttered as I walked to the table. I gazed down on the old man. "You did a nice job. He looks peaceful."

"It doesn't matter. The family wants the casket closed." She grunted as she adjusted four straps around Mr. Engelhart, then buckled them expertly into place.

Behind her on the wall were two buttons. She pressed

one. I heard a soft hum, the slack was taken up, and Mr. Engelhart rose off the table. His legs stuck straight out, as though he were a magician's levitating act. I had a wild desire to giggle. Poor old fellow. Dangling from the ceiling like a mobile.

"Stand back until I get him closer to the casket," cautioned Margaret.

She pushed the other button. With a jerk, Mr. Engelhart floated on his way, but it was not a dignified process. It seemed to me that the entire system needed an overhaul. The machine stalled twice. These abrupt stops and starts made Mr. Engelhart jiggle and swing.

"Should I steady him?" I asked.

"He's secure as long as I don't take the pulley up too far. I think I broke some teeth out of the wheel when Mrs. Devinski died. That woman weighed four hundred pounds. Best cook in Woodgrove, but she must have sampled everything she made. I had to order a specially built casket for her."

How mortifying! I ran my hands down my slim hips and vowed to leave those damned cheeseburgers alone. No special-ordered casket for this old girl.

"Okay," said Margaret. "He's as close as we can get him. You take his shoulders. I'll stand here in the middle. We'll heave him over the side."

Heave? Not a word I wanted to think about while grasping a dead man's shoulders in a room where mysterious things happened.

I was facing the counter and saw a metal box sitting beside the sink. The manufacturer's nameplate identified it as an embalming pump. Fastened to the top of the box was a clear canister with numbers and level measures. The entire contraption was plugged into an electrical outlet. Loops of black rubber tubing coiled on the floor.

The cabinet above the sink held an assortment of scalpels, picks, and other instruments that looked painful. One, especially, caught my eye. It looked to be made of stainless steel and was twelve inches long. The handle was molded to fit the grip of a hand. The pointed end was wicked.

"Well?" said Margaret impatiently. "What are you waiting for? He isn't going to help us."

I nodded to the cabinet. "What's that?"

"What's what?" replied Margaret, glancing around.

"That long tool there in the cabinet."

"Trocar. Tool of my trade."

I chuckled. "In my husband's line of work it would be classed as a deadly weapon."

She rolled her eyes and asked curtly, "Are you ready?"

I put my hands under Mr. Engelhart's shoulders. "I guess so. On the count of three?"

"Whatever."

"One. Two. Three," I said, and gave the body a boost up. I was pleased. I'd done my part. Mr. Engelhart's upper torso was almost in, though he was hardly in a position that would meet with his family's approval. Margaret huffed and puffed, but she wasn't making headway.

"Want me to come around there?" I offered.

"No. Stay there. He's heavier than I thought. I had Joseph's help earlier." She wiped a hand across her brow. "You steady him. Don't let him fall. I'm going to raise the hoist."

"But I thought—" I stopped. I can get myself into the damnedest messes. All I'd wanted was the answers to a few questions, and here I was, wrestling a dead man into his casket. A fine Sunday morning pastime. Behind me the motor whirred and Mr. Engelhart made a jerky leap into the air.

"Stay with him," instructed Margaret. "Keep him steady. Bend over more, so you can get a better hold. Don't let him sway away from the casket. I can't remember how high—"

I didn't hear what she said because the winch made a series of high-pitched shrieks. Everything happened so fast. One minute Mr. Engelhart was suspended above me. The next he was falling. I tried to move, but his head cracked into mine. He didn't feel any pain. I wasn't as lucky. A bright light exploded behind my eyes, then a black curtain of unconsciousness dropped into place.

Chapter Eight

The floor of an embalming room is hard and cold.

"Never state the obvious," I whispered. Carl had been fond of quoting those words. Originally, they'd been said by his army drill sergeant, but they'd found their way into most of Carl's observations on life.

I forced my eyes open. I must not have been out long. Margaret was coming toward me with a folded towel in her hand. When I focused on her, she flung the towel into the sink.

"You're awake," she said.

Again, the obvious. I could see her. My eyes must be open. Some wayward thought nudged my tender brain. I blinked and slowly sat up. With gentle fingers, I explored the lump on my head. "If that's a cold compress," I murmured, "I could use it."

"Let me help you up," she said and grasped me firmly by the arm. "I'll get you some ice."

She hauled me to my feet. I swayed weakly. My wavering gaze settled on Mr. Engelhart. Poor old guy. He appeared to be making a desperate attempt to flee his eternal home. His legs stuck over the edge of the casket; his face was buried in the pillow.

"Are you going to leave him like that?" I asked.

Margaret shrugged. "I'll get him situated later."

It didn't seem right, but I'd had enough of embalming rooms, caskets, and bodies to last me a lifetime. Which, judging from the headache that pounded behind my eyes, could be ending sooner than I had planned.

The smell of the room was making me nauseous, or maybe it was my throbbing head. Whatever the reason, I needed out of this confining space.

I waved away Margaret's offer for ice, accepted her apology with a nod, then wished I hadn't. Dizziness forced me to close my eyes.

"You don't look very good," she said. "Come lie down."

"Air," I mumbled. "I need fresh air." I shook off her helping hand and stumbled out the door and down the corridor.

From behind me, Margaret asked, "Where are you going?"

Dazed, I repeated, "Going?"

"Yes. Are you going home?"

I looked at Margaret and saw lines of worry etched around her eyes. Was she thinking lawsuit? She had nothing to fear. I didn't want anyone to hear this morbid tale. "Now, you mean?"

"Of course, now. Should you be driving?"

Oh, yes. I should be in my car and driving the hell

away from this place. But I didn't say that. "I'll be fine," I replied.

"But what if . . ."

I blocked her out so I could concentrate on getting the door open. I was unprepared for the blinding sunshine that blazed in my face. I caught my toe on the threshold and nearly plunged headfirst out the door.

Margaret was close by. I felt the brush of her fingers on my arm, but I hurried out into the warm, bright light. I wobbled down the sidewalk to my car. With a studied effort, I fumbled the key into the ignition. When the motor was going, I put the car in gear and pulled away. But only to the next block. Out of sight of the funeral home, I parked and rested my head on the steering wheel.

I lowered my window and took several deep, cleansing breaths. Each time I exhaled, my thoughts grew clearer. The rapid beating of my heart was losing speed. My head ached, but it was a dull, bearable pain.

For a while, I drove aimlessly around Woodgrove. The day had a nice nip. After the stale air in the funeral home, it was invigorating. It made me appreciate just being alive. A breeze in my open window carried the scent of meat roasting over a charcoal fire. My stomach rolled. I wasn't hungry. In fact, my stomach churned with anxiety, but I wasn't sure why.

I drove down the deserted main street looking at the buildings. Most were in good repair. A few needed a coat of paint to spruce them up. Woodgrove has a hardware store, a bank, a feed store, a grocery store, a lumberyard, and a small library.

On impulse, I pulled into a parking spot and stared at the library. In my early years, I'd spent hours among those shelves of books. Today, it was closed. I knew I'd have to come back, but for the life of me, I couldn't remember why. Two doors down was the Pin Oak Café. Judging from the lack of cars in front, service wouldn't be a problem, and conversation with a local waitress might be informative.

I left my car and walked to the café. My headache had eased, but if I touched the bump, pain radiated out like fiery spokes on a wheel.

"Then don't touch it," I muttered as I reached for the café doorknob. It was jerked out of my hand, and I stared at Cecil Bellows.

When he saw me, his expression changed. The wrinkles in his face deepened. His mouth drew up; his lower lip pooched out. He looked like a disgruntled bulldog. He slammed the door behind him and took me by the arm.

"We're going to talk, little lady." He laughed. "Never figured on using that word to describe you. Little? Ha."

I pulled my arm from his grasp but followed him away from the café. Cecil had on his usual bib overalls. Since it was Sunday, he'd traded his blue chambray workshirt for a festive plaid. He was big and beefy. His work boots were caked with mud, his hands massive, the backs covered with brown liver spots.

"What did you want to talk about?" I asked.

"What are you doing here? Every time I turn around, I see you. What's your business?"

Whatever it is, it's none of yours, I wanted to say. Instead, I shrugged. "I miss the old hometown. It's a pretty day for a drive." I stared him in the eye. "Take your pick."

"Bah!" he spluttered. "You didn't come here for the weather. You're a snoop. A troublemaker. We've already got Sid. We sure as hell don't need you."

"Did Sid question you? Are you a suspect? Did that nasty temper of yours get out of hand?"

"Why you—"

"See?" I grinned knowingly. "Possible. It's surely possible. You don't like the Millers. You don't like me." I opened my eyes wide. "Should I be scared of you, Cecil? Will you use that nasty old temper on me?"

His face darkened to a dull red. "Your mother would be ashamed of you," he muttered. Shaking his head, he walked to his truck parked down by the feed store.

He was right. Mom would be ashamed. She hadn't liked Cecil, but she'd always treated him courteously. She'd said Edna had a hard enough life without any of us aggravating Cecil. I'd done more than aggravated the man. I'd taunted him about being a suspect in a murder investigation.

Carl's voice chided me. "If you move too quickly, Bretta, you'll alienate all your resources. Besides, Babe, you're ticking people off."

I looked down the street and saw Cecil sitting in his

truck glaring at me. I hurried into the café, hungry for human companionship and thirsty for a tall, icy glass of lemonade. I had my choice of seats at the counter. I took one by the door. At a back table, two waitresses were puffing away on cigarettes.

"Be right there, sugar," called the blonde.

Her hair was swept up in a tall do and sprayed rigidly into place. A pair of miniature dice dangled from her earlobes. She hopped up, then bent over to smash out her cigarette. I saw a tiny butt and spindly legs encased in lemon yellow spandex. She didn't wear an apron but had tucked her order book in the pocket of her floral-printed blouse. "What'll it be, cookie?" she asked, moving behind the counter.

"Do you still make fresh-squeezed lemonade?" I asked, then couldn't resist. "Bubbles?"

Her head jerked up. Her eyes widened as she studied my face and recognition dawned. "Bretta? Is that you?"

I nodded. She and I had gone to high school together. Her real name was Melvinna Hixson, but we'd nick-named her Bubbles because she seemed to float aimlessly through school.

" 'Course we do. Why, honey, you look like a million bucks." She took a lemon from a basket and rolled it across the cutting board. Her fingers went about their task, while her eyes took in my hot pink shirt, the di-amond studs in my ears, and the ring Carl had given me when we'd gotten engaged. She added water, sugar, and ice to the lemon juice and set the glass on a napkin in front of me with a flourish.

I wasn't surprised when she came around the counter and plopped down on the stool next to mine. She gave me a broad wink and said, "I heard you were around."

I took a sip and sighed blissfully as the tart drink slid down my parched throat. "Let me guess. Cecil?"

"Old fart. Don't have a good word to say about nothing or no one."

"Some things never change," I remarked.

"You have. Girl, you look great. Ten years younger. You make me feel like a grandma." She laughed. "Which I am."

"Really?"

"Five times. 'Course, I take care of myself, exercise, watch my calories." She gave me a long look. "But I don't have to tell you about that." She pointed to my ring. "I see you got married."

"I'm a widow. Carl died a little over a year ago. What about you?"

Bubbles flashed her ring finger under my nose. I caught a glimpse of a tiny diamond. "I'm engaged. I've been married three times," she said cheerfully, "but the fourth time is the charm for me. I'm making this one last."

She looked around with a fond smile. "I'll miss this old dump. I always come back here when my marriage ends."

"You're leaving Woodgrove?"

Bubbles crossed her fingers. "Real soon, I hope."

We'd covered the pleasantries; now it was time for

some information. Remembering Carl's advice, I tried for subtlety. "You'll miss all the excitement. What with the murder and all."

"Don't concern me. Amish aren't big on coming in here." She leaned close and whispered, "They don't tip worth a damn."

I turned my head away from her stale, smoky breath. "This place used to be gossip central. Has it changed?"

"Nah, we still get the same old coffee drinkers. Whoever said women are the talkers should spend a morning in this joint. These old guys can debate everything from politics to abortion, and to hear them talk, they're the authority on it all."

"What're they saying about the murder?"

She toyed with a stiff curl. "You'd think conversations would be buzzing, but I haven't heard much of anything."

"Strange."

"You bet. This town has an opinion on everything. Most of the people around here tolerate the Amish, but they don't become friends. Everyone knows someone, even does business with them, buying eggs or vegetables in season. Here at the café, George has a standing order for pies, bread, and rolls. They're brought to the back door four times a week."

"I can't believe no one has speculated on who'd kill an Amish man." I picked an ice chip from my glass and popped it into my mouth, the picture of innocence. "What do you think?"

"He must have done something. You don't go through this old life without stepping on someone's toes. He must have pissed someone off."

"Don't you wonder what happened?"

"Not really," she admitted, unconcerned. She smoothed her shirt front. "I've got me a wedding to plan. I figure white is out of the question, so I found me a beige dress. You know, symbolic like. A soiled virgin." She hooted. "That's me, cupcake. Soiled, but I enjoyed each and every minute."

I sipped my lemonade and nodded at her tacky but innocent rambling. Bubbles she'd been, and Bubbles, I saw, had never changed. She was still drifting along. As I drained the last of my drink, I wished her success with this marriage and handed her a ten-dollar bill. She started over to make change, but I told her to keep it as a wedding present.

"It was great seeing you," I said. "If you need a bride's bouquet for your wedding, give me a call. I have a flower shop in River City."

She was in the process of tucking the extra money into her bra. Her hand froze over her breast, and she gave me a wide-eyed stare. "Say, I bet that's why you're here in town. The Amish man's flowers." She shook her head. "Too bad, honey. My Leray says he has that deal in the bag."

I touched my bottom lip with the tip of my tongue, then worked at keeping my voice normal. "Leray?"

"Yeah, Leray Hodges. Why, cupcake, didn't I tell you about my honey? He's just a big old sweetie pie."

I shook my head slowly. With all this talk of honey, cupcakes, and sweetie pie, I was going to need an insulin shot to combat the sugar rush. "Does he live around here?"

"Sure does. Lives at the edge of town for now. Later we plan on moving, just as soon as he makes that kill-ing—"

Her voice trailed off. "Lord almighty. Bad choice of words, what with that murder an' all." She giggled. "If my sugar bear can get the widow to agree, we'll be living on easy street but in another town. All the roads in Woodgrove have potholes and dead ends."

Chapter Nine

I came out of the café to find Leray's green van parked at the curb. I wasn't pleased to see him leaning against the rear of my car. He had one arm across his belly, the other elbow propped on it. He was picking his nose with his little finger.

"A real sugar bear," I muttered as I walked toward him. He'd traded his patched jeans for a pair of ill-fitted dress pants. The pleats in front were puffed out like the guy was glad to see me. He immediately let me know that wasn't the case.

He rubbed his little finger down the side of his leg, then nodded toward the café. "What were you doing in there?"

"It's lunchtime," I said.

"Other places to eat. Try River City. I hear they have restaurants."

"And I hear congratulations are in order. You're a busy man. Engaged to Bubbles. Engaged in all kinds of deals. Does Moth know you're working at cutting him out of Isaac's flowers?"

"Heard you'd been to see him. I ain't the only one who's been busy."

I shrugged. "My day off. I get around. See people. Talk."

Leray's eyes narrowed. "Cute. You think you're damned cute playing detective. Won't get you nothing but trouble."

"From you?" I asked.

"Maybe. Maybe not."

"You're the one who's going to be in trouble if you're working both ends toward the middle. I'd hate to have Moth *and* Allison on my back."

"Whaddayou mean?"

I leaned against the door of my car. "Allison asked me to go in with her and the other florists. The plan is to offer the Miller family money for Isaac's flowers. But Moth says he had an agreement with Isaac. He seems confident that he has the rights to everything Isaac grew. Where does that leave you and the florists?"

Leray snorted. "Moth don't have squat. As for that Thorpe woman, she's more into organizing and running over people than she is the facts."

"What facts?"

"That without me, none of them have diddly. I'm the one Isaac trusted. I'm the one the family will listen to."

I cocked an eyebrow. "Oh, really? Didn't look to me like they were ready to jump at the deal you were offering."

"They'll understand," he replied with a sly smile, "once they see the whole picture."

"What is the whole picture?"

"Just you never mind. Isaac and me had some long talks. He was coming around to my way of thinking until last week." Leray scowled. "Them Amish are damned funny. Dealing with them is like walking through a field of cotton candy in a rainstorm. One minute, you're walking on clouds. The next, you're up to your ass in goo."

"What happened?"

"How the hell should I know?" Leray pushed off from my car. "Gotta go pick up my woman." His round face split with a grin. "She's a fine thing. Fine thing. Got our evening all planned out. A little mood music, a grilled steak, a mess of parsnips, crusty French bread, a glass of wine, and who knows what'll happen?"

Parsnips? The king of romance.

I tuned him out. His blathering was bringing my headache back. Damn, my brain was acting strange. Cotton candy. I could see great mounds of it floating before my eyes. A conversation with Leray was like eating some of the stuff. On the surface it looks filling, but take a bite and it's only fluff.

He was talking about the parsnips, telling how his mother used to cook them. I interrupted him to say, "Flowers die without attention. Who's taking care of Isaac's?"

Leray stared at me. I didn't like the look in his eyes. I reached behind me and opened the door. "It isn't a secret," I lied. "I see your plans slipping away. Too many people are involved. You aren't alone in this. Not anymore."

He took a step toward me. I jumped in the car and locked the door.

"Listen to me," he shouted. "Evan said he'd hear me out after Isaac's funeral. I have first say. Hear that? I have first say about Isaac's plants."

As I left, Leray was glaring maliciously after me. I pressed icy fingers to my hot cheeks, trying to calm down. He was a man desperate to protect his interests. Exactly what they were, I hadn't a clue.

I left Woodgrove with my mind in a jumble and a lump on my head. Several questions had been answered, but another set had cropped up. I decided to drive by Evan's and see how many buggies were in the yard. I needed to talk to him. I wanted to make sure Sid hadn't done anything rash, like arresting Evan for Isaac's murder.

I'd seen the gleam in Sid's eyes. I'd heard the determination in his voice. Evan had messed in a murder investigation—Sid's investigation. Sid is smart. Evan is naive. Sid might feed Evan too much rope, hoping the Amish man would hang himself. Evan, trying to co-operate, might unintentionally slip the noose over his head.

With a death in the family, I wasn't sure if Evan would attend church. I knew the services were held at a different Amish home each Sunday. A special wagon carried the wooden benches from house to house as the service moved around the district.

I slowed down as I approached Evan's home. It looked deserted, the doors shut. The buggy was gone from the shed. I coasted by Isaac's house and was surprised to see Evan sitting alone on the front porch. I applied the brakes, backed up, and pulled in.

Evan came slowly to his feet. He moved across the grass like an old man. His skin was sallow, his eyes haunted.

I got out of the car and stood quietly, waiting for Evan to look at me. When he did, I asked, "Can we talk?"

"Everyone's gone to church. I stayed with Rosalie and . . . Isaac." He drew a deep breath in through his nose but let it out through his mouth in a weary gust. "I have to stay close," he explained bitterly. "The sheriff told me not to go anywhere."

For the first time that day, I smiled with genuine amusement. "Evan, Sid didn't mean you couldn't move out of the yard. He just doesn't want you to hop on a plane and fly away."

Evan ducked his head. "Yeah, but I figure I'd better toe his line."

We walked to the porch and sat on the steps. "I guess Sid's been talking to you," I said.

Evan's cheeks flushed above his beard. "Yesterday he took me into River City to his office. They didn't bring me home until after dark."

The man was embarrassed. I was moved to touch him on the sleeve. "Sid has a job to do. He has to ask questions. I imagine he thought he'd get straight answers if he took you away from these familiar surroundings."

Evan hung his head. "It was mortifying to be carted off." He glanced at me. "I didn't do anything wrong, Bretta. When I found Isaac in the field, I thought he'd slipped off the wagon and hit his head. There was a cut. Not much blood. It was only when I picked him up that I knew his neck was broken."

He rubbed his work-roughened hands together. "Years ago, we had a colt that was as wild as a March wind. I was trying to herd him into the barn, but he went crazy and ran into a plank fence. I was fifty feet from him, but I heard the crack. He'd broken his neck."

The rasp of Evan's hands rubbing back and forth sounded like sandpaper. He sighed softly. "It was the same with Isaac. When I picked him up, his head flopped just like that colt's."

"That's why you didn't call an ambulance?"

"I didn't see what they could do. He was already cool. We take care of our own. We bathe them. We dress them. Until a few years ago, we didn't involve a funeral home at all."

Evan lowered his eyes and shuddered. "I guess I didn't know what autopsy meant until I saw what they did to him. I dressed him. Only me. Rosalie wanted to be there, but once I saw—" He gulped. "I took care of him. She won't ever know. Ever."

Tears pricked my eyes. "I'm sorry, Evan. Sorry for all of this. I wish there was something I could do."

"There is."

"What?"

Evan's voice vibrated with emotion. "Find out who killed Isaac. Find out why all this is happening. I feel like my life is—" He held out his hands helplessly. "The sheriff thinks I'm hiding something. The only thing I haven't told him is that Katie saw someone in the field with Isaac. I've talked to her, but she doesn't know who it was. She was in our garden. Isaac's field is up on the hill. Her eyesight is poor. She'll get glasses after I harvest the corn."

"Maybe she's mistaken."

Evan shook his head. "No. She's sure, and I believe her. Someone was with him. You find out who, Bretta, then maybe the sheriff will let us bury what's happened when we bury Isaac tomorrow."

We were silent, each lost in thought. I gazed up at the maple trees that shaded the yard. The wind played hopscotch across their tops. Sometimes the leaves danced as a strong breeze touched them. Then the wind would die down, and a gentle puff of air would make them tremble flirtatiously.

I brushed a strand of hair out of my eyes and asked, "Who called the sheriff that night?"

"Margaret Jenkins. When we had Isaac ready for her, I went to Sam's to use his phone. While I was gone, Katie told Cleome of seeing someone with Isaac. When Cleome repeated the story to me, I was uneasy. But Isaac was dead. There wasn't anything we could do."

"So, it was Margaret's decision to call in the sheriff?"

"I told her on the phone that we'd washed Isaac and had him ready for her. She was upset. I didn't understand why. When she got to the house, she explained that when someone has been ill, what we did might be okay. But Isaac was strong, young, and healthy. The authorities had to be called in. She'd taken care of that before she left Woodgrove. They arrived right after she did."

"Why didn't you tell me all this yesterday?"

Evan lifted one shoulder. "Don't know. I guess even then I thought it was a misunderstanding, or I hoped it was. The sheriff says murder. Isaac's neck was broken. He was struck down with a piece of pipe."

"Pipe? What kind of pipe?"

"The sheriff didn't say, other than it was rusty. Flecks of rust were found in the wound on Isaac's head. The sheriff brought a paper that gave him the right to look through all my junk and in the barn, house, and sheds. It didn't matter to me. I gave him the paper back and told him he hadn't needed to type it up. He could look wherever he wanted."

"Search warrant," I murmured. "I guess he didn't find anything?"

Evan studied me. "There wasn't anything to find."

"I know, Evan. But whoever killed Isaac could have planted"—seeing his puzzlement, I amended—"could have hidden the murder weapon on your place to put the blame on you."

"Why would anyone do that?"

"Why would anyone kill Isaac?" I countered. This was the opening I needed. "Unless it had to do with Isaac's work. What's he been doing?"

"Growing flowers. Planning a new greenhouse. Studying his books."

"Books?" I murmured. There it was. "When we talked yesterday, you said Isaac had things on his mind. Have you given any thought as to what they might be?"

"Too many things on *my* mind to think about Isaac's thoughts."

"Could I see these books? Maybe they'd give me an idea."

"You could, except Rosalie sent them with Cleome to drop off at the library."

"What kind of books did Isaac check out?"

"About plants, growing, fertilizers, propagation." His tongue stumbled over the last word. "We always called it taking slips."

"Propagation? What was he propagating?"

"Some old plants that've been around for years. Rosalie knows. Sometime you'll have to get her to tell you."

I couldn't wait for sometime. I needed answers now. "Would she visit with me while I'm here?"

"She's lying down. I don't want to bother her. Tomorrow will be hard on her. In the next hour, our families will begin to arrive from Illinois and Indiana for the funeral. They should have been here last night, but one of the vans they hired had engine trouble. They had to stop to get it fixed."

"How long will they stay?"

"Two or three days."

Two or three days—too much time would have passed. "Tell me about the plants, Evan."

"Not much to tell. Isaac kept the mother plants on a table in front of the greenhouse. Inside are the new starts. They're just a bunch of plants, to my way of thinking."

"They're not just a bunch of plants," Rosalie said from behind the screen door.

I sprang up and turned around. She stepped out on the porch but kept the door open. She looked tired, her eyes red-rimmed, her face wan.

"Did our talking disturb you?" I asked.

"No. But I want you to understand about Isaac's plants."

"I'd like to hear about them."

Rosalie's lower lip quivered, but she steadied it. When she had control, she explained, "They're special. They weren't bought from strangers. They're part of our heritage. Some of them date back generations."

"What kind of plants?" I asked.

"All kinds. My family are direct descendants of the first Amish to come to Lancaster County. Those people brought plants from their homeland, and each time a son or a daughter married, several different slips were given to them. When I became Isaac's wife, my mother gave us our starters.

"My husband loved having those plants because they had a history of coming to America with Jacob Ammann, our Amish founder. Isaac said the plants are a tough strain because they've survived over three hundred years."

Tears filled her eyes, and she pulled a handkerchief

from her sleeve. "They're not just plants. They're part of my life with Isaac." She cradled her bulging stomach. "They're something my children and I can cherish." She turned and went into the house. The door closed.

I looked at Evan. "Can I see these plants?"

He shrugged. "I guess so. Why?"

"I don't know. Just curious."

Evan flashed me a ghost of his old smile. "And people think we Amish are strange."

Chapter Ten

I'd tried to coax Evan into coming with me to Isaac's greenhouse. But I left him on the porch, convinced that he had to follow Sid's order. I sighed. Dealing with someone's death is painful under any circumstances. For that death to be murder, and for a peaceable man like Evan to know that he's suspected, was more than he could comprehend. Add in the complications of living by the Amish faith in a world structured for our modern society, and he was out of his depth.

Carl had thought Sid a good sheriff. A good detective. So why was I involved? Was Margaret right? Was I lonesome? Sometimes. I sure as hell didn't think I was better than Sid at deduction, but my methods for seeking the truth would differ from his.

This community had been my community. I knew these people. I'd grown up with most of them. I'd shared meals with them. I didn't know how much Sid knew about them, or if he was prejudiced against the Amish. Was his mind open to all possibilities? What if he was looking only for evidence to convict Evan? I couldn't let that happen.

Sid would boil me in oil if he knew what I was thinking. If he knew what I was doing . . . well. I swallowed uneasily. That thought was as welcome as my annual trip to the gynecologist.

The holding shed was my first stop. I opened the door. No windows, and no plants. Gravel on a dirt floor. Empty except for some buckets stacked in a corner. I pulled the door shut and went to the greenhouse.

The entrance was covered by an awning. Sitting on a makeshift table underneath was Isaac's collection of plants. I looked them over carefully. None were growing in clay or plastic pots. A bushy fern had its roots in a discarded aluminum roaster; an old blue granite teakettle was home to a striped airplane plant. Two handleless saucepans held a Christmas cactus and a shamrock plant. The table was white enamel. At first glance, it resembled a kitchen stove. With the assortment of pans on top, it looked as if someone was cooking up a chlorophyll meal guaranteed to bring on a case of photosynthesis indigestion.

"Get a grip," I said aloud.

I touched the lump on my head. Painful. I'd been having weird thoughts since butting heads with Mr. Engelhart.

The greenhouse was approximately forty feet long and was sunk in the ground up to the eaves. Air currents carried hot, moist air up the five steps that led down into the pit. The glass roof slanted up to a ridge cap, and along the top were hinged windows. Since the day was warm, most were cranked up for ventilation.

Inside the greenhouse, the temperature was comfortable. The walls that supported the roof were made of cement blocks. A central walkway ran the length with a bench on each side. The steady drip of water plopping into a bucket was the only sound. No fans. No motors. No automation.

Hodges could rest assured. The plants were being cared for. Everything was wet. In fact, someone had watered recently. Drops caught the light and glittered on the lush green foliage. On my left was a huge wood-burning stove. Two long sections of clay tiles formed a flue that ran from the stove under the benches.

I walked down the path on the lookout for something spectacular. A rare specimen. I was afraid I'd see it and not know. I can identify a ficus, a philodendron, a bromeliad, or a dracaena, but those are standard flower shop varieties.

I was looking for miraculous. All I saw were young starters from the plants outside on the table. Near the back was a roped-off section of chrysanthemums. Not a particularly unique flower. I got to the end of the walk and started back.

I glanced at the roof and was dazzled by the sun reflected on the glass. I searched behind the stove, in the stove, among Isaac's supplies lying neatly on a few shelves. I went up the steps to the houseplants and snooped among their healthy foliage. I came back down befuddled.

All the other plants were lumped together except for the section of chrysanthemums. These plants were in all stages of growth—an old plant in a cast-off dishpan, cuttings that didn't have roots, small plants with new foliage, large ones with buds but no blooms. Each neat row was labeled with numbers: 3–15–97. 8–21–97. 1–12–98. 5–14–98. 9–5–98. Were these propagation dates?

"Think," I commanded myself.

Moth had spoken of "anything Isaac Miller had a hand in growing." Isaac had been studying propagation—the reproduction or multiplying of a plant. To my inexperienced eye, Isaac had been reproducing new chrysanthemum plants from the mother plant growing in the dishpan. The dates showed he'd been keeping a record. None of the other plants had tags with dates.

I gave the mother plant a closer inspection. I poked at the dirt. It was firm. I tried to pick it up, but it was too heavy.

Why all the interest in Isaac's plants? Leray said that once Evan saw the whole picture, he'd understand and would cooperate. Bubbles said she and Leray would leave Woodgrove and be on easy street. That sounded like she was expecting a comfortable life. Money?

I went down the aisle for the third time and stopped again at the budded chrysanthemum plants. Lots of tiny nubs crowned each sturdy stem. In a few weeks they would be bursting with color.

Like a thief, I cast a furtive glance around, then pulled off a bud. Carefully, I eased a fingernail under the thin membrane that held the petals in place. The tiniest bit of color. Dark. I popped off another bud from a different plant. Same deep hue. After several more, I decided there weren't any yellow, lavender, or white among Isaac's plants. All were dark. But not burgundy or purple. Bronze? I didn't see any brown tones. More like red.

A shadow crossed the glass above me. I jerked my head up so fast, the world took a nosedive. I clutched the bench and peered blindly at the dark figure towering over me. My heart pumped like a piston in a race car. All that was between us was a thin sheet of glass. It offered me little protection. One well-placed blow, and I would be showered with razor-sharp shards. Before I could think, small fingers tapped lightly on the glass.

I shaded my eyes and saw Katie. The air passage to my constricted throat opened, and I took a much-needed breath.

"Hi," I called weakly. I motioned for her to come to the door of the greenhouse. I got the impression of a shy smile, then the shadow melted away.

I looked around one more time. It irked me that Moth and Hodges knew more than I did. It left Evan wide open to be hoodwinked by a pair of greedy men. Perhaps it had even cost Isaac his life.

Katie was waiting for me when I came up the steps. I grinned at her. "What are you doing?" I asked. Her answer was low and bashful.

I stopped rubbing the telltale plant stains off my fingers. So there would be no misunderstanding, I repeated what I thought she'd said. "Your father told you I was here?"

She nodded.

I paused to let this news sink in. Evan had sent his daughter to me. Nothing odd about that. Evan knew I liked Katie, enjoyed visiting with her. But he also knew I wanted to talk to her about the night Isaac was killed. Was this his okay to question her about what she'd seen?

For a minute I was overwhelmed with a flood of emotions. There could be no bigger demonstration of trust than what Evan was giving me. But with that trust came responsibility. What if I upset Katie? What if I asked or said something that frightened her?

I'd been silent too long. Katie was puzzled. A frown marred her brow. Her blue eyes became unsure. She was dressed like a miniature Amish woman. Dark dress and apron, white devotion cap tied under her chin. Legs covered with heavy stockings, feet encased in thick-soled shoes.

I touched her on the arm and asked her the first thing that popped into my head. "How was church?"

Katie didn't know how to answer this ridiculous question. She finally whispered, "Fine."

"Evan says company is coming." She flashed me a grin. "Lots of cousins to visit with?"

While we had this one-way chat, I searched my brain for a way to introduce the subject of the person in the field. Another thought occurred before I could think how to phrase my questions. Did Cleome know Katie was with me? That spurred me on.

"Katie, Evan tells me that you saw someone with Isaac the night he died?"

Her first full sentence filled me with alarm. "I should have gone up there," she said.

"Oh, no. You did the right thing in telling your mother. Did you recognize who it was?"

"No, I've been thinking and thinking. It was just a figure. It was almost dark. I was in the garden picking some cucumbers that I'd missed."

I chucked her under the chin. "Cleome sent you back out, didn't she. My mother used to do that. I'd pick and pick, but she'd come along behind and find another bucketful that I'd missed."

Katie's eyes widened with amazement. "That's what happened," she admitted. "I'd gotten to the end of the row and was going to the house. But I stopped to look at the flowers. They're pretty in the evening with the last bit of sun on them."

She turned to Isaac's field. "Men were up there most of yesterday. Their feet crushed some of the blooms." Her tone was sad. "That's exactly where they were that night."

Doors slammed. Loud voices carried to us from the house. The company had arrived. Katie's head swiveled around.

"Go on," I encouraged her. "We'll talk another time."

She hesitated long enough to say, "You told me once

that you used to go for walks to the creek. Will you go with me the next time you visit?"

"I'd like that very much. We'll plan for it after your company has gone home."

Satisfied, Katie skipped ahead. I followed at a more sedate pace. When I rounded the corner of the cutting shed, I stopped to stare in fascination at the scene before me. The driveway looked as if it had been invaded by a flock of excited blackbirds. Amish women scurried back and forth from three vans to both houses. They carried babies, suitcases, and covered baskets. Their voices rose and fell as they called to each other. Men stood under the trees, their faces solemn, their beards identical in size and length.

It took me a minute to pick out Evan. Three of the men had to be his brothers. The resemblance was remarkable. I moved into view. All conversation came to an abrupt halt when they spotted me. In my hot pink shirt and blue jeans, I stood out like a preening peacock.

Taking a self-conscious breath, I crossed the driveway. Evan looked from me to Katie. He gave a slight nod when he saw the smile on her face. His eyes caught mine in a slow, steady gaze. What transpired between us was as vocal as conversation, though not a word was uttered. I hadn't been mistaken. He'd sent Katie to find me on purpose. His faith and trust in me were startling. My steps faltered.

Cleome broke away from a group of women, her mouth tipped up in a smile. Once her back was turned, and only I could see, that smile faded. She crossed to me and said, "It's time for you to go."

"I'm leaving. But would you tell Evan—"

Her eyes narrowed. "Now isn't the time to talk."

"I can see that." I spoke evenly. "Tell Evan not to sign anything. Not to make any quick decisions about Isaac's plants."

Cleome's frown vanished. "I'll tell him, but it won't make any difference. He's decided to plow the flower field and sow wheat." She favored me with a hint of a condescending smirk, then walked away.

Under the watchful gaze of thirty or more pairs of eyes, I couldn't do or say anything that might embarrass Evan. I got in my car and drove down the road to Sam Kramer's. His was a long lane, the house out of sight behind some trees. I parked and sat.

Suddenly, I pounded the steering wheel in frustration. Once again Evan had neglected to tell me something important. Why? First he hadn't told me about moving Isaac's body from the field. Now he hadn't told me about his decision to plow up the flower field. Had he conceded this point to please Eli Detweiler? What of the plants in the greenhouse? Rosalie would be crushed if they were destroyed; but if Detweiler kept at Evan, would Evan give in?

Wearily, I shook my head. I didn't know what to think. If the plants were gone, Moth and Hodges would be incensed. That gave my declining spirits a boost, but it didn't last.

If the plants were the motive for Isaac's murder, they had to be preserved. Which brought up the subject of Sid. What was I going to tell him? Or did I need to talk to him at all? Perhaps he and his men had already made these connections.

I doubted it. My marriage to Carl had taught me many things about police work. One was the fact that officers of the law doggedly follow the same procedure. Question the suspects. Look for inconsistencies. Check alibis. Nine times out of ten, the motive for murder is anger, jealousy, or greed. Sid might look for greed, but only in an obvious way. I couldn't picture him in the greenhouse plucking off flower heads and wondering at the bud formation on a bunch of chrysanthemums.

Through the windshield, I gazed up at the sky. Softly, I said, "I need a sign that I'm on the right track. Could you . . . uh . . . help me out here?" Afraid that I might be taken literally, I added, "No bolt of lightning. Just something I'll recognize."

I waited. Nothing happened. I sighed. What had I expected? It was Sunday. His day off.

Chapter Eleven

Human activity around the Kramer homestead was nonexistent, but the animals were going strong. A dozen chickens scratched under shade trees. Ducks and geese heralded my arrival with frantic honking. The billy goat that had journeyed to Cleome's garden was tethered to a fence post. His bucket was on its side. A dark pattern of moisture had spread across the dry, barren ground.

I stood next to my car and stared. My jaw should have hung in disbelief, but I kept it clenched. The smell of livestock was overpowering. The flies were so thick, I worried that something might pop uninvited into my mouth if it was open.

The house had never been much, but time and little upkeep had taken it farther down the path to ruination. The front door was boarded over, its porch minus most of its floor. Windows were askew. The foundation was crumbling away, bringing the structure to its knees.

Years ago, the place had been considered an eyesore. Today, that would have been a compliment. Evidence of Sam's get-rich-quick schemes was scattered around the yard. Cars, rusted and abandoned in tall weeds, had been disemboweled, the parts sold for a quick buck or two. Aluminum cans, tossed haphazardly in and around four fifty-gallon barrels, waited to be taken to a recycling center. Lawn mowers and garden tillers sprawled like wounded soldiers on a battlefield, their crankcases bleeding oil, their usefulness a dim memory.

Among the trees was a row of empty, dilapidated rabbit hutches. The whole town knew that Sam had bought a herd of rabbits, planning to breed them and sell the offspring for slaughter. Sam had seen dollar signs every time he'd put a doe in with Elmo, a fine, lop-eared old buck. Elmo had serviced his herd with energy; he'd humped away with glee. But he didn't produce any babies. The rabbit was sterile, as well as a carrier of a disease akin to gonorrhea in humans. By the time Sam figured out something was wrong, his entire herd had been infected. The community had gotten a big laugh at Sam's expense. All agreed that only Sam would invest in a rabbit that had a venereal disease.

I approached the back door cautiously, sidestepping alternate piles of manure, hunks of iron, and scraps of lumber. I didn't have to knock. The door opened as soon as my feet touched the creaky porch steps.

The only time I'd seen Sam in anything but overalls and the dingy long underwear he wore winter and summer was at my mother's funeral. He'd arrived in a black suit that had smelled of mothballs and been covered with a powdering of green mold.

"Hello, Sam," I said.

A feisty seventy-five, Sam was tall and thin. He had a head of hair a younger man would have envied, though time had changed it from black to gray. His teeth were false and too big for his mouth. He worked around them until they were in place.

"Who are you?" he demanded.

"Bretta Solomon." I helped him make the connection. "Lillie McGinness's daughter."

"Lillie?" He spoke my mother's name softly, almost devoutly. "Miss that woman," he declared. He reached into his pocket and brought out a pair of Kmart's finest black-rimmed glasses. He pushed them over his ears and studied me, cocking his head first one way and then another.

"Don't look like Bretta to me," he declared.

"I've lost weight. How are you?"

"Can't complain," he muttered, eyeing me as if I were a bug stuck on a pin. He pronounced judgment. "Liked you better the other way. A woman needs meat on her bones. Gotta have a place to grab hold." He heehawed with such vigor that his upper teeth flipped out. Quick as a lick, he caught them and wallowed them around until they were situated.

"Want to come in?" he asked. "I just fixed up a kettle of turnip greens and ham bones." He sniffed the air. "Oh, boy," he said, smacking his lips. Instinctively, I ducked, just in case his teeth decided to make another exit. "Don't it smell good? Makes my old stomach rumble."

It made my stomach revolt. Eat with Sam? Talk

about diet control. I quickly said, "I have to get back to River City." I mumbled something about an appointment. "I stopped to ask about your neighbor, Isaac Miller."

"What about him? He's dead unless them Amish have a way of resurrecting him." He tee-heed. I waited. "That Isaac was an odd one. Lived in a fine house on some of the best land around, and what does he grow? Flowers."

Sam shook his head disdainfully. "It beats the hell out of me how he came up with the idea. Must have been a good one. Heard tell he was sitting on a gold mine."

"Did Isaac tell you that?"

Sam lowered his voice and looked around suspiciously. I wondered if he was afraid a chicken might overhear. "Me and Isaac weren't exactly on friendly terms. He didn't like old Saul"—he nodded at the wayward goat—"munching on his flowers."

"Did you have words?" I asked sympathetically.

Sam grunted. "More times than you can count. I told him someone was letting Saul out of his pen. The man didn't believe me. I don't blame old Saul for running off to them Amish. They keep their soil fertile and loose." He quirked an eyebrow at me. "Kind of like their women."

I jerked back as he bellowed, but this time Sam covered his mouth with a grimy hand. I swallowed uneasily. The combination of Sam's cooking, the piles of manure, and plain old filth was pushing bile up my throat.

"Why would someone let Saul out?" I asked.

"Don't know."

"Did you ever see anyone? Hear anything?"

"Nope. I camped out a time or two. But nothing happened."

"Was it in the daytime or at night?

"Both. No rhyme or reason to it. 'Cept it caused me trouble with the Millers."

"Did you see Isaac the night he was killed?"

"See him?" Sam repeated. A light dawned in his nearsighted eyes. He adjusted his glasses. "You've lost more than fat if you'd ask me such a question. I know my place, and it's here. Seems to me you have a place, too."

It was a dismissal. I was only too glad to comply. At the end of the driveway, I weighed my options. I could drive back to River City, close myself up in the flower shop, and tackle the paperwork. Or I could keep driving, asking questions. The day was nice, the paperwork boring. I wasn't sure if I was making any headway, but it was more exciting than adding and subtracting columns of numbers. I decided to take the gravel road that circled behind Evan's place, then head for home.

It had been years since I'd traveled this route. I approached the house where the widow Arnette used to live. She'd passed away. I wondered who'd taken over the property, then knew they were Amish once I got closer to the house. The windows were curtainless, and several pieces of horse-drawn farm equipment sat in a neat row outside the barn.

Detweiler was the name on the mailbox. I pulled to the side of the road and stared at the house. A dog tied to a tree set up a howl, but I assumed no one else was home. I was proved wrong when I heard the back door slam. An Amish woman came into view. She had a pan in her hand and was headed for the dog. She turned to see what was bothering him, and I got out of my car and walked toward her.

I assumed this was Mrs. Detweiler. She was a thin wisp of a woman. When I was within talking distance, I saw her face was flushed, her eyes watery. She dabbed at her nose with a white handkerchief.

"I didn't hear you drive up," she said nasally. She hushed the dog with a sharp command. He fell quiet, but his eyes rested eagerly on the pan.

"I stopped when I saw the name on the mailbox. Are you the bishop's wife?" At her nod, I said, "I'm Bretta Solomon, a friend of the Millers."

I didn't expect her to know who I was, but the timid smile on her lips dissolved when she heard my name. She stammered, "I . . . I . . . What do you want?"

I'd never thought of myself as a threat, but this old woman clearly saw me as one. She shrank away from me as I tried to make myself seem harmless, neighborly. She sneezed, and I asked, "Are you ill?"

"Horseweed is in full bloom."

She kept eyeing me. It was uncomfortable to be found

intimidating. What had she heard? Who had told her to be wary of me? I was sure it was her husband. She sidled a step further away when I said, "I met the bishop at Rosalie Miller's. Apparently, he and Isaac were having trouble."

"No," she said quickly. "Not trouble."

"They didn't agree about the flowers. How do you feel about them?"

"Why I . . . I . . . Eli knows best."

Nothing more than I would have expected from a faithful Amish wife. I looked across the road in the direction of Evan's farm and Isaac's field. The flowers weren't visible, but I could see Evan's barn roof.

I turned a smile on Mrs. Detweiler. "What a convenience for you. By crossing that fence you can visit Cleome without getting out on the road."

"I don't go much, especially this time of year. The pollen bothers me."

"But your husband uses that shortcut, doesn't he?"

Avoiding my question, she set the pan on the ground. The dog lapped at the food hungrily. With both hands free, Mrs. Detweiler fretted nervously with the handkerchief. She looked past me and kneaded the fabric frantically.

In the back of my mind I must have heard the steady *clip-clop* of a horse's hooves. I'd been preoccupied with framing my questions, so the sound hadn't registered. But when I turned, Detweiler was there in his buggy in the driveway.

He didn't raise his voice, but his words came easily

to my ears. "You *will* leave my wife alone. You *will* get off my property. It is written by our Lord, Second Thessalonians, chapter three, verse eleven: 'For we hear that there are some which walk among you disorderly, working not at all, but are busybodies.'"

I refused to show this man any emotion. I nodded politely to Mrs. Detweiler, then moved without hurrying to my car. I climbed in, took time to fasten my seat belt before switching on the engine. With my shoulders squared, I drove away.

Chapter Twelve

I cruised up a hill and down the other side before my embarrassment gave way to anger. Eli Detweiler was an intimidating man. He might wield power in the Amish community, but he didn't have anything over me. I should have demanded answers. I should have bullied him as he'd tried to bully me. But that might have caused trouble for Evan. I didn't want that. Evan had enough to deal with.

I eased off the accelerator as I entered a tunnel of trees. The shifting leaves created a mosaic pattern of light and dark on the graveled road. With the sun blocked, the temperature dropped ten degrees. My tires picked up rocks and flung them against the undercarriage of the car. The sound grated on my throbbing head. My stomach let me know it had been too long since my last meal.

I steered through a tight S-curve, then rattled over a bridge spanning the creek that flowed onto Evan's property. I thought about my promise to Katie, that soon, we'd take a walk. Then I worried that the wrong person might discover she'd seen someone in the field with

Isaac the evening he was killed. I wondered if I should warn Evan not to tell anyone, but I didn't want to burden him with yet another worry.

Isaac's flowers were on my right. On the other side of the road were acres and acres of row crops—Cecil Bellows's pride and joy. He lavished time and money on his land the way some people indulge their children.

Cecil farmed a total of seven hundred acres, of which two hundred was pasture. Evan's entire farm was eighty-five acres. Cecil's horsepower belched diesel fumes. Evan did his work with a team of horses.

The Bellows' house sat back from the road and was like everything Cecil owned—big and showy. I slowed when I saw his truck was gone. Edna was in her vegetable garden. When she heard my car, she straightened to shade her eyes with a dirt-crusted hand.

I pulled into the drive and called out the window, "Hi, Edna. You're really giving them old weeds hell."

She came toward me with a smile of welcome. Though she was slight in stature, her delicate appearance was deceiving. I'd seen her hop on a tractor while her brawny husband manned another, and they would disk a field together. Today, she had on a broad-brimmed hat, saucy green scarf circling the crown and tied in a bow under her chin.

Her gaze was frank and friendly. "Bretta, I saw you yesterday at Evan's. I wanted to visit, but you know Cecil." She touched me on the arm. "You look wonderful, dear. Your mother would be so proud, and a few days ago I was by your flower shop. The windows are lovely. Such artistic talent."

"Thanks," I murmured. "Is Cecil here?"

"Gone to town. The coast is clear. Want to come to the house for a cup of coffee and a piece of pie?" She gave me a teasing look. "Or do you still eat coconut cream?"

A wave of pure longing swept over me. Edna's pies were to die for. But so was being caught in her kitchen if Cecil came back before I'd left. I smothered the urge to go in with her. I told her I was on my way home.

She didn't try to hide her disappointment. "I get lonesome. I miss your mother, Bretta. She understood so much."

I knew what she meant—Cecil. Everyone in the entire town cringed when they saw him coming. It didn't allow Edna much of a social life when everyone shied away from her husband.

I was tempted to reconsider, and not just for the piece of pie. I liked Edna. I knew she'd enjoy the company; but I also remembered the way I'd baited Cecil.

"Maybe another time. Right now, I stopped to ask you about Isaac's death."

She stammered in surprise, "Uh, me? What ... uh ... could I know?"

"Did you hear anything unusual the night he was killed?"

Edna frowned. "I worked in the garden until dark. I like to pick my green beans late in the evening, break them while I watch television, then can them the next morning."

"Mom did, too," I said. "While you were out here, did you see a car or a truck go by?" As an afterthought, I added, "Or a van?"

"Probably. Someone is always churning up dust." She motioned to the lime-covered grass and weeds. "I'll be glad when it rains."

"Who was it?"

"Who was what?" She looked confused, then that cleared and she answered, "Gosh, I don't remember who went by."

I motioned toward the trees across the road. "Did you hear any voices coming from Isaac's field?"

"Sounds do carry at night. If the wind is right, I can hear Cleome call her family to supper."

"What about the night Isaac was murdered? Did you hear anything?"

She peered in the car window at me. "Sid asked me the same questions, Bretta. Why are you repeating them?"

I didn't need to search my brain for an explanation. The words were there on my tongue, and I knew they were the truth. "I was married to Carl for twenty-four years. In his work, questions are asked all the time. I guess I've taken on the habit."

Edna nodded. "Yeah. I know what you mean. Forty-seven years of being married to Cecil has changed me, too. I catch myself screaming at the cows when they misbehave. I used to talk real gentle to them." She sighed. "I'll tell you, like I did Sid. I heard loud voices, but I didn't pay them much attention. I do remember thinking it was odd to hear anger coming from the Millers'."

"Can you tell me what was said?"

"Oh, no. All I heard was a raised voice a couple of times."

I persisted. "Anything, Edna. A word, even?"

" 'Stop' was used a couple of times," she replied softly. Closing her eyes, she concentrated. "I heard someone say 'stunning.' " She opened her eyes. "You know, like Isaac's flowers were stunning."

"Was it a man or a woman's voice?"

"I assumed it was a man. I really thought it was Evan, that he and Isaac were having a disagreement."

"Evan?" I gulped. "Are you sure?"

"No. I'm not. I'm not sure at all. I just thought it was Evan because I don't know who else Isaac might've had words with."

"So you didn't actually hear Evan's voice? You just thought it might be him?"

"That's right. Who else could it have been?"

"Whoever killed Isaac."

She jerked back in surprise. "Bretta, you're not looking for the murderer!"

We both heard tires leave the blacktop road and hit the gravel. "Edna," I asked quickly, "does Cecil still go to his Moose meetings on Thursday nights?"

She made a face. "Come hell or high water."

I glanced at the road. The vehicle was getting closer.

I could see dust fogging the air. "Was he late getting home that night?"

"No, same time. About ten."

I saw a flash of red through the trees. "Did Cecil ever argue with Isaac?"

Her face closed like a hibiscus bloom at dusk. She turned her eyes toward the red truck that streaked into the drive. In a dull voice, she said, "I see what you're getting at, Bretta. You'd better go. Cecil is a cantankerous man, but he isn't a killer."

For his seventy-odd years, Cecil could move fast. He was out of his truck and striding toward my car before I had the engine started. I put the lever in reverse and pushed the pedal to the floor. My tires spun. Gravel flew. I skidded toward the ditch. I eased up on the gas and wrestled the car under control. Cecil didn't follow me to the road, but my window was down. I flinched at his words.

"I'm reporting you, Bretta. Sid's going to hear about this harassment. Your ass is grass, and I'm going to mow you down."

I put as much space between us as I safely could on the gravel road. When I stopped at the blacktop, I didn't have to consider my next move. Home. I'd made enough enemies for a Sunday. Fact was, I'd made enough for the next year.

Carl's laughter echoed in my ears. "You've got potential, Babe, but you lack finesse."

My spirits were glum as I traveled the few miles to the site where the boys had been killed. As I approached the spot, I coasted along. The wreath was still there. So was the black ribbon tied around the trunk of the tree. Without considering why, I pulled over and stopped.

I opened the glove compartment and took out the packet of money. I untaped the end and sniffed. The odor was still discernible. Had I smelled that aroma on anyone today? Not that I could recall. I put the bag back in the glove box.

I turned my attention to the land opposite the accident. Mutinous cedar trees had jumped the road ditch and were making a valiant effort to survive in the rocky soil. Their counterparts had sunk their roots down deep and were a lush green. The hot afternoon sun released their spicy fragrance.

Evan had told me Sam thought someone was letting the goat out of his pen, and Sam had confirmed it. Why let the goat loose? Unless it was to wreak havoc on Isaac's flower field.

I got out of the car, crossed the shallow ditch, and worked my way up the rocky slope onto the edge of Sam's property. I didn't know what I was looking for, but something had made those boys miss the curve. Perhaps it was inexperience on a winding road. Or maybe a vehicle had been parked in the way. The proximity of the accident to Sam's property was bugging me.

I stood at the top of the ridge and gazed down at my car, at the angle where the boys had gone off the road. With the hill and the curve, it was a treacherous place. Add a parked car, or someone getting in or out of one, and I could see where the driver might have swerved.

Add inexperience and excessive speed, and the results would be devastating.

But why would anyone park here? To deliberately let Sam's goat loose? The boys had been killed on Monday evening. Isaac had been killed late Thursday. I pushed brush aside and walked through what Sam might have called a fence. The wire hung in limp strands. Gaping holes big enough for an elephant made it easy for me to trespass.

The ground was covered with rocks. The thick canopy of trees had kept the undergrowth from sprouting. I walked in a straight line from where my car was parked. The dirt didn't show prints. I had no way of knowing if someone had passed this way recently.

It took me less than five minutes to reach the clearing around Sam's house and barn. While still some distance away, I could see him feeding his animals. I thought about the motive behind Isaac's death. I thought about the people involved, both directly and indirectly, in his life and his flowers.

Leray and Moth both wanted whatever Isaac had. Sam had said that Isaac was sitting on a gold mine. Cecil craved power. In most people's minds, money was power. Where was the source of this money going to come from?

I rubbed my forehead. I was too tired to think. Rotating my head, I tried to ease the tension from my neck muscles. A sharp, shooting pain made me moan softly.

The pain led my thoughts back to Margaret. Her occupation might go a long way toward explaining her oddness, but not all the way. Subscribing to the Amish magazine seemed a bit extreme. The part she played in an Amish burial was minimal. Embalming someone of Amish faith wouldn't be any different from embalming a Catholic or a Baptist.

A car slowed on the road behind me. It stopped. I took two steps in that direction. All I needed was for my car to be cited as an obstruction or for it to cause an accident. But then I heard the car speed off.

I paused to look back at Sam. He'd untied old Saul and was trying to entice him into a pen. From my vantage point, the pen appeared to be sturdier than anything else on Sam's property. Sam shook a bucket. The goat didn't show any interest.

I was losing mine, too. I'd started for my car when I heard tires chew gravel voraciously. I turned toward Sam's place and saw that the sheriff's car had led a group of patrol cars to a dust-choking stop in his yard. Sid was out first, followed by a troop of his men. I scurried behind a tree to watch.

The goat made a break for freedom. Sam started after him but stopped abruptly. I was too far away to hear, but whatever had kept the old man from giving chase made him furious. He gestured toward the vanishing goat.

Sid stomped his way to Sam and produced a piece of paper. Impatiently, everyone waited while Sam went through the motions of pulling his eyeglasses from his overalls pocket. He adjusted them on his nose. Peered at the paper. Looked at the other men.

"Search warrant," I murmured. Why Sam's place?

Sid spread his arms to encompass the entire area. His men hesitated. I smiled. Searching for anything on Sam's place would be worse than looking for the proverbial needle. I settled myself for a long wait, but ten minutes later a deputy gave a yelp of success. He pulled a plastic bag from his pocket, fussed about with it on the ground, then held up a two-foot length of pipe.

The murder weapon? Evan had said Isaac was struck down with a piece of pipe. I studied Sam Kramer. He seemed more concerned with the goat. Sid put the pipe under Sam's nose. Sam reached for it. Sid jerked it away. Was Sid accusing Sam of murder? Sam flapped his arms vehemently.

I couldn't hear anything, but I'd seen enough. I wanted out of the area and to be on my way back to River City before Sid had a chance to see me. I left the thicket, slid down the rocky slope, and leaped the ditch. I hurried to my car, which I'd left unlocked. I was sure I'd left the window down, but it was rolled up now.

Strange, I thought, as I opened the door and hopped in. Just as I'd figured, the afternoon sun had heated up the interior. I squirmed as the vinyl seat burned through my jeans. I started the car and switched on the air conditioner. Pressing on the accelerator, I gathered speed quickly. I leaned over and checked the glove compartment. The money and letter were still in their plastic bags. I sighed my relief.

My thoughts returned to what I'd just witnessed at Sam's place. It was damned odd to me that among all the trash that surrounded the property, the sheriff and his men would so quickly find the murder weapon. Or was it merely a piece of pipe? I'd seen plenty of scrap iron lying around.

A rustling in the backseat startled me. I glanced over the seat but didn't see the source. It sounded like cellophane. I flipped off the blower for the air.

There it was again—a slick, delicate riffling of movement over crisp paper. A few days ago, I'd dropped the wrapper from a sugar-free cookie on the floor. Was that it?

"Mouse?" I groaned. "Could a mouse get in my car?"

I hate mice. What if it crawled up my pants leg?

I glanced down and thought my heart would stop. I saw a forked tongue tasting the air and beady eyes staring up at me. A snake was crawling out from under the passenger seat.

Chapter Thirteen

My first impulse was to hit the brake pedal, but I was doing sixty miles an hour. Was the snake poisonous? Would it strike if I moved my foot off the gas and onto the brake? Maybe knocking heads with Mr. Engelhart had done more damage than I'd thought, and the snake was only an illusion.

I looked down. Nope. Still there.

My brain felt wrapped in cotton, my mouth dry with fear. I didn't know what to do. I sure as hell wasn't going to drive the remaining miles to River City with a snake.

Sid.

Where the hell are the cops when you need 'em? They had guns. They could shoot the . . .

A movement caught my eye. The snake was on the prowl. His head shifted from side to side. His tongue flickered.

I cringed, afraid to breathe. Most of his body was still under the seat. How long was he? His head appeared enormous. But that could've been fear magnifying the size.

He stretched his neck toward my legs. If he crawled under my feet, I was done for. I was afraid to move my foot to the brake. What if the motion excited him?

"Think," I muttered wildly. "What do you know about snakes?"

Panic brought sweat to my forehead. Moisture trickled down my back. Pee running down my legs would surely be next.

Pit viper. Could I see any pits? I was afraid to look. Rattlesnake? No diamonds, no sound. Cottonmouth water moccasin? Didn't want him to open his mouth so I could check. Copperhead. They were plentiful around this rocky area. No copper color. This snake was black and tan with light-colored rings across its back.

Snakes are cold-blooded. Warm air makes them active. Would cold air . . . ? The controls for the air conditioner were close at hand. So was the snake. More of his body had slithered from under the seat. The vent was aimed at him. If I could just . . .

Sharp curve.

I wrenched the steering wheel. My speeding tires squealed a protest. I gripped the wheel tighter. Which was worse? An accident or a snakebite?

Damn. It was a hell of a choice. I eased my foot off the accelerator. The movement caught the snake's eye. He glided forward until his head was draped over my shin bone. I could feel his weight.

A whimper rose from my throat. Not all of his body was visible, but there was enough. Over four feet long.

While he was occupied with my legs, I slowly worked

my right hand to the temperature control. Gently, I flipped on the air. A blast of cold hit my damp face. I pushed the fan switch up to MAXIMUM and looked down through the spokes of the steering wheel.

The snake wasn't affected by the lowered temperature. His restlessness was aggressive, his interest in his surroundings keen. I tipped up my toes, taking more pressure off the gas pedal. The shifting of my leg muscles was minute. But he felt them. His head arched. We stared at each other, then I had to give my attention to the road.

I'd gradually cut my speed to thirty. I was past panic. I'd entered hysteria. I considered driving on the wrong side of the road, opening the door, and flinging myself out into the weeds.

Pain upon landing, possible broken bones, and a car that would be a total wreck kept me in my seat.

Just ahead, a car turned out of a side road. It was Sid. Behind him the other patrol cars waited for me to pass. I needed to get their attention. I employed an age-old, tried-and-true method: I flipped them my middle finger.

It worked. They pulled behind me. Red lights flashed on. I released my seat belt.

This was it. If the snake hadn't bitten me by now, perhaps it wasn't the biting kind. It was a chance I had to take.

Sid's brake lights came on. He was pulling over. I had help behind me. I had help in front of me. I had a snake draped across my legs. The air inside the car was frigid. How fast could a snake bite? How fast could I slow my car and leap out? If he was poisonous, at least I had an army of police to get me to the hospital. Ditto if I broke an important part of my anatomy.

I tensed, then threw caution to the wind. In one movement, I slammed on the brakes and opened my door. The car was still moving when I rolled off the seat and hit the pavement.

I tried to cradle my head, to take the brunt of the impact on my arms and shoulders. Hot pain shot through my body. Squalling tires on asphalt screamed in my ears. I heard a crash. Then dead quiet.

Was I alive?

Suddenly, a string of profanity filled the air. I didn't figure God allowed that kind of language in heaven. Slowly, I opened my eyes.

Blue sky. Sticky tar under my head. I moved my arms. Wow! Too much pain to be dead.

"Holy shit, Bretta," said Sid, standing over me. "What the hell kind of trick was that?"

Instead of answering, I pointed a shaky finger toward my car. The crash I'd heard had been my own driverless vehicle rear-ending his. The impact had swung my door shut. Two feet of the snake's body had been caught between the door and its frame. He wasn't dead, either. His mouth was open. His body writhed viciously.

The sight was more than this woman could handle. Let Sid piece it together. With a sigh, I sank into oblivion.

• • •

I spent the night in the hospital. No broken bones. Bruises, abrasions. My body felt like it had been forced through a meat grinder. At some hazy point, I'd opened my eyes to find Sid at my bedside.

I didn't endear myself to him when I asked, "Is my car totaled?"

"No. And I'm fine, too, Bretta. 'Course, Sam Kramer is threatening a lawsuit against Spencer County. Whiplash. Severe neck injuries. But don't let that interfere with your recovery."

"Sue the county?" I mumbled. "I'm the one who hit you."

"Yeah, that's right. Store that piece of information in that thick skull of yours in case you have to testify."

I drifted off. I must have imagined that he picked up my hand and gave it a light squeeze. Not Sid. He was too damned tough to show affection, though I'd seen tears in his eyes at Carl's funeral.

I was dismissed by the doctors at noon on Monday. Was Isaac's funeral service over? I took a cab to my house and found my car parked in the drive. The front fender was crumpled. Something brown was smeared on the white paint of the driver's door. I shuddered and turned to the porch. Yesterday's paper lay by the front door. Wonder of wonders. My sore muscles protested as I bent to pick it up.

I entered the house and headed straight for my room. I hadn't called anyone except Lois to tell her I was in the hospital. She had offered to bring me clothes and to visit. I hadn't wanted either. At the hospital, I'd worn one of their stiff, sterile gowns. Now, all I wanted was a full-length mirror, a hot shower, and my soft robe.

I moaned and groaned as I stripped off my clothes. In dismay, I stared at the bruises and scrapes. My body isn't great in good times; too much fat under the skin for too many years had left ugly stretch marks. The bruise on my hip was monochromatic blues and purples. But the raw places on my elbows were what really hurt.

I took a quick shower, washed the antiseptic smell from my hair, and stepped on the scales. I'd lost three pounds in the last couple of days. Murder was a grim appetite suppressant. Wrapped in my robe, I hurried down the hall, past the closed door. I was always conscious of the master suite, though I tried to tell myself the room had ceased to exist the night Carl died.

I yearned for a hot fudge sundae topped with pecans and whipped cream. I settled for a low-fat pizza and popped it into the oven. While I waited for it to heat, I dialed the Woodgrove Library, a number etched in my memory since childhood. I asked that any book Isaac Miller had checked out in the last three months be set aside for me to look at tomorrow.

The young lady on the phone didn't think that would be possible. I told her to tell Miss Ginko that the request came from Bretta McGinness Solomon. I made sure she had the name spelled correctly and hung up.

Next, I called the flower shop and talked to Lois. Our conversation was brief, since it was the third one we'd had that day. I told her I was taking her advice. I would be off work until noon tomorrow. If she needed help, she could call one of the part-time designers. After she'd told me to check under my car seat, mind my own business, and drink plenty of orange juice, I replaced the receiver.

Orange juice? I shook my head and took a deep breath. The next number wasn't as easy to dial. Slowly, my fingers found the digits. Someone answered on the first ring. I identified myself and asked for Sid.

His voice was in my ear faster than I'd expected. "What now, Bretta?" he grumbled.

"What kind of snake?"

"A young python."

"Not a native to Missouri fauna, right?"

"Hardly."

"Is it dead?"

"Yeah."

"Did you find the murder weapon?"

Without missing a beat, Sid replied, "Car door did him in."

"What?" I said, then grimaced. "I meant the weapon that killed Isaac."

"I know what you meant. What do you know about a murder weapon?"

"Well . . . I . . . you said in the hospital Sam Kramer was in your car. I figured you'd found something and were taking him in for questioning."

"Not bad deducting," admitted Sid. "Carl used to say I should . . ." He stopped, then to my amazement, he volunteered information. "Sam isn't a strong suspect, but we had to check out an anonymous tip we received."

"Phone or mail?"

"Mail."

"Typewritten?" I asked, thinking of the order for the wreath.

"Yes," said Sid.

"Who'd know the pipe was there except the murderer?"

"Not bad. I wonder why that hadn't occurred to me?" he said sarcastically. "What else have you surmised?"

"The snake didn't get in my car by itself."

"Doubt it. Don't you lock your doors?"

"In River City. Not Woodgrove."

"Whose toes have you been stepping on, Bretta?"

I'd been doing a regular Mexican hat dance on everyone's feet, but I ignored his question. "Did you know J. W. Moth of River City Wholesale Floral has a snake? Check him out, Sid, see if he was around Woodgrove yesterday. My car was unlocked and parked . . ." I came to a grinding halt. If I listed all the places I'd been, I'd be giving Sid an itinerary of my entire day. Not a good move.

"Yes?" he drawled. "Go on. Where were you parked and what the hell have you been up to?"

"Oh. Here and there. This and that."

He snorted. "I hope you've used some of those brilliant deducting powers to realize that whoever put that snake in your car was hoping to bring you grief. The snake wasn't poisonous, but its creeping around the floorboards could've led you to have a serious accident."

"I know. If he'd crawled out about a mile or two back, when I was into all those curves, I might not be sitting here having this conversation with you."

I paused for a second, then asked, "When those boys were killed on the curve, did the Highway Patrol suspect something, and their suspicions didn't reach the public?"

Silence.

"I have to know, Sid. Were there questions?"

"Those boys are dead and buried. Speculating will cause the families nothing but more heartache."

"So there were suspicions?"

"Yes," he admitted reluctantly. "Skid marks didn't jive with the path the car would have taken if it was just traveling too fast to make the curve. The patrol officer figured the driver came around the curve, saw something, probably a deer. He swerved, lost control, and that was it."

"Like hell."

"What?" demanded Sid. "You aren't thinking that kid found a snake in his car?"

"No, no. Of course not."

"Then what are you doing raking this up?"

"Just thinking."

"Yeah, well, when you get to thinking, you give me a pain in the . . . head. I'm hanging up now. I have work to do."

"Motive, Sid. Why was Isaac murdered?"

"Time's up. Just because I'm called a public servant

doesn't mean I'm here to do *your* bidding."

Click. He was gone.

Before I could be annoyed that Sid had been so rude, I smelled something burning. "My pizza!"

I slammed the phone down, hurried to the oven, and pulled the door open. A cloud of smoke billowed in my face. I choked and fanned the air. The cheese had turned to a smoldering, glutinous mess, the crust a fine ebony. I grabbed the pizza with a hotpad and tested it with a fork. The pizza was ready—ready for the trash.

Irritated, I dumped it into the bin and searched in the refrigerator. I needed to go grocery shopping. It had been days since I'd stopped for more than a quart of skim milk and a loaf of bread.

"What to eat?" I muttered. The cold air from the refrigerator swirled around my bare ankles. The sensation brought back memories of the snake. I slammed the door and leaned against it. Holding my head in my hands, I slid down until my rear end rested on the floor.

In the hospital, the medicine had kept my thoughts out of focus. Since coming home, I'd forced them away. Now they rushed in, bringing back all the fear and hysteria.

I'd been told I was cool-headed, that I'd reacted with common sense. But now a sob worked its way up my throat. Self-preservation makes the weak strong. Makes the strong desperate. Makes the desperate . . . murder.

I'd poked in a murder investigation. I'd poked until I'd annoyed the culprit. I'd made him feel that I was to be feared. That I needed to be stopped. I wiped my face on the sleeve of my robe and almost smiled.

I'd asked for a sign so I'd know if I was on the right trail. As a child, I'd been cautioned not to wish for something unless I was prepared for the consequences.

I'd wanted assurance that I was on the right path. Well, I had it. I was on that path. The path of a killer.

Chapter Fourteen

I rarely take an afternoon away from the flower shop, so I decided to make the most of it. I fixed a cup of hot chocolate, added some marshmallows for my sweet tooth, and curled up on the couch. With pen in hand, I made a list of everyone I'd talked to on Sunday. When I was finished, I was amazed at the length.

"Busy, busy," I murmured. "Busybody," I amended, thinking of Detweiler's quote.

Was I? You damned betcha. That snake had clinched it. B.S.—Before Snake—my activities hadn't really hurt anyone except the guilty person. I chewed on the cap of the pen. How long had the snake been in my car? I shivered. The vehicle I'd heard while I'd been on Sam's property was my best bet. I was certain I'd left the driver's window down. It was up when I came back.

My eyes traced the letters of a name I hadn't considered as a suspect. Edna Bellows. She said she'd been by my flower shop. Had she pushed the order for the wreath under the door?

I leaned against a pillow and remembered when I was a kid in 4-H Club. Edna had taught a class on snakes. The boys had been thrilled because it was much more exciting than woodworking. I'd had a crush on one of the guys and considered trading sewing for snakes. I'd given it some serious thought, but the boy's dimples didn't have that much attraction. I'd stayed with my needles and thread; of course, that hadn't done me any good either.

Where would Edna get a snake? And not just any snake but a python? Where would anyone get it? Unless they already had one in their possession. Moth. If he had one snake, he could have two. Would Sid talk to him?

I struggled to my feet and went to the phone book. Pet store. I looked in the Yellow Pages. Eight stores. I rolled my eyes but dialed the first number. I didn't have anything better to do. I wasn't ready to get in my car and take a drive.

The first four didn't sell snakes. On the fifth try, I struck pay dirt. "I was wondering if you sell snakes?" I began.

"Yes."

"Pythons?"

"Yes, we do." His voice deepened as he employed his sales pitch. "Regardless of their bad publicity, snakes, especially pythons, make excellent pets."

"Yeah, right."

My attitude wasn't that of a prospective customer. The brightness in his voice dimmed. "Lady, I'm busy. If you're interested, we've got three in stock."

"What about food?"

"Yeah, they eat. Mice, rats. Depends on the size of the snake."

I squeezed my eyes shut on this image. "Who buys them?"

"Snake owners. Look, I—"

"Can you give me their names?"

"Are you kidding? We don't give out that information. Besides, there are over thirty."

"Thirty people have snakes?" I squawked.

"That's just from our store," he boasted. "Of course, we do specialize in reptiles."

"J. W. Moth," I said.

"Good customer. Are you a friend of his?"

The lie came easily. "Sure."

Respect came across the line. "He's steered several friends our way. Come on in. I'll personally see to it that we find the right snake for you. What's your name?"

Impulsively, I answered, "Edna Bellows."

"All right, Edna. When you come into the store, ask for Rodney."

"How about Margaret Jenkins?"

"What?"

"She told me to call you, too."

"Fine. Is she a customer? Did she get a snake here?"

On a roll, I decided to push my luck. I asked, "How about Hodges?"

"Leray? Sure. Great guy. Loves old Arnie, his python."

I hung up. Moth and Leray. Why wasn't I surprised?

Leray had been leaning against my car when I came out of the café. Leray Hodges. A snake owning a snake. But that didn't fit. The salesman had said Leray loved Arnie. Why put something you love, even a snake, in a car with someone who would destroy it, given the chance?

I glanced at the clock. Almost three-thirty. Time for the paperboy. I took up my position at the window so I had a clear view of the street. Yesterday, he'd tossed the paper on my porch. What would he do today?

I peeked out the window. I'd learned from my neighbors that Jamie delivered the papers between three-thirty and three-forty-five. It was getting close to that. I leaned forward.

Five minutes later, I saw the biker. He had refined his work to a fine art, each movement accomplished with precision. Feet on pedals. Knees against handlebars to steer. Hands free to grasp papers from the basket and toss them. Pedal, reach, toss. Pedal, reach, toss. I was impressed.

He came down the street at a good clip until he got to my house. His feet stopped. His eyes swept the house.

Suddenly, I remembered my car visible on the drive. "Hell and damnation," I muttered. "He knows I'm home."

The bike wobbled. I stared at the kid. Very overweight. Sloppy clothes, black jogging pants, huge T-shirt. A ball cap pulled low on his forehead. He tossed the paper. I heard it hit the porch. With a burst of speed, he picked up his synchronized movements and rode on. I kept watching, saw him glance over his shoulder, then he was gone.

Disgusted, I chastised myself, "If you're going to catch the kid in the act, have the smarts to pull your car into the garage."

I stepped out on the porch, picked up the paper, and brought it inside. Back on the couch, I flipped it open. Nothing new. Probably just as well. I was too tired to think, too tired to move. I fell asleep over one of Allison's newspaper ads. I could only hope other readers had done the same.

I woke at eleven, stumbled to the bathroom, and brushed my teeth. I got into bed and drifted back to sleep. Eight hours later, I awoke to clouds hiding the sun.

It would have been easy to stay in bed. I'd told Lois I wouldn't be in until noon. But I had things to do. I creaked out of bed, inspected my scrapes, and checked to make sure the automatic coffeemaker had started brewing.

After a shower, I reached for a pair of jeans, then changed my mind. Jeans wouldn't impress a proper, eighty-year-old librarian. With Miss Ginko in mind, I put on a dark green skirt and print blouse. On the way out of the bedroom, I grabbed the matching jacket.

I filled a travel mug with coffee, grabbed an apple, and headed for the car. Lois had told me to check under the seats. I didn't think I'd ever get in a car again without first making an inspection. All was clear.

I stopped for gas a couple of blocks from home.

While waiting my turn to pay, I worked hard at ignoring the Hostess cupcakes that were within easy reach. Maybe just one. I had a strong hankering for the gooey center. Besides, I'd lost three more pounds. I moved up to pay. There was still time to grab a package.

Stella, the cashier, leaned across the counter and eyed me from head to toe. "Damn, you're looking good, Mrs. Solomon. You're a real inspiration for the rest of us chubbies." She rubbed her rounded tummy. "I'm gonna have to do something about this before people start thinking I'm pregnant." She clicked some keys on the register. "That'll be twelve dollars, unless you want something else."

I shook my head and smiled at her. "Thanks, Stella, but the gas is it." As I walked out the door, I called back to her, "And thanks for the compliment. I needed to hear that this morning."

My spirits were high until I left River City. With each passing mile, my nerves were giving me fits. This same posture—hands in the ten and three o'clock positions, leg extended to the accelerator—brought total recall. I kept glancing at the floorboards. I kept remembering the weight of the snake on my leg. My hands shook for the better part of the drive to Woodgrove.

I parked at the library, secured my car, and walked in. I was disappointed to find an unfamiliar face at the front desk. When I identified myself, I was told that Miss Ginko was home with the flu. A stack of books was passed to me, along with a short note.

I carried the books to a vacant table and sat down to read the note. It said:

Bretta,
I'm sorry I missed you. According to my records, Isaac checked out the book on mutations five times in the last three months. Come see me, again.

Regards,
Olive Ginko

I tucked the note in my pocket and saw that the book she'd mentioned was on top. It was old, the pages frequently thumbed. A section near the front didn't lay flat. I inserted a finger and eased it open. It was a chapter entitled "How to Recognize a Sport."

"Sport?" I mumbled.

I read on quickly. A sport is a plant showing marked variation from the normal type, usually as a result of mutation. Using the index, I looked up "mutation." "Any hereditary change in a character not due to crossing." This is not something that a grower develops. A mutation is a freak of nature.

For three-quarters of an hour, I pored over the book. I learned that mutations happen for no explicable reason. There is no limit and no predictability to the changes that occur spontaneously in a plant. But it's never the entire plant. A single stem can mutate. From this mutant, other plants can then be propagated.

My interest perked up as I read: "Mutations seem to

occur at a certain stage in a plant's age or history. The new form may be entirely different from the mother plant."

History . . . mother plant? My mind sorted through all the information. Rosalie had said Isaac's plants had a history of nearly three hundred years. Did age have to do with the mutations? Was the mother plant in the dishpan one of the plants with a special history?

Around me, housewives dropped off books and visited by the front door. My concentration was jarred by preschool children asking questions in shrill voices. I wanted to plug my ears. They wouldn't be so noisy if Miss Ginko was here.

I turned to the other books. The subjects included construction of greenhouses, ventilation, soil types. It looked like routine stuff. In the last book, I found a brief section on propagating mutations. Quickly, I read through the procedure: trays of cuttings; young plants with new growth; older plants ready to bloom.

I'd seen plants like these in Isaac's greenhouse. All were chrysanthemums. All had been cuttings off the parent plant that had been growing in a discarded dishpan. Had that plant mutated?

I needed more information, but this tiny library wasn't the place to get it. I put the books on the corner of the desk and walked out to the sidewalk. Where could I get more information on what seemed to be a rare occurrence? Since mutations are rare, did that mean they're worth money? If so, how much? Isaac had been propagating chrysanthemums. Why? Had he seen wealth in the future? Or had he done it for the pure joy? Maybe both, I decided, thinking how he'd cared for the plants because of their lineage.

I already knew Hodges and Moth wanted what Isaac had. But how much did they know? I thought back over my conversations with them. Moth had said, "*anything* Isaac Miller had a hand in growing." He'd been covering all his bases. Hodges had said, "I have first say about Isaac's *plants*." As a florist I should have caught the specific use of the word "plants" instead of flowers. In my mind there's a difference. Apparently, others had made that same distinction. Moth wouldn't answer any of my questions; neither would Hodges, but there was another possibility.

My gaze settled on the Pin Oak Café door, which kept swinging as customers went in for early coffee. I followed an old man in and found the café a far cry from the way it was on Sunday. The place was crowded with customers; not a seat left in the house. Silverware clanked against plates, and the smell of bacon frying and hot coffee made me salivate.

I looked for Bubbles but saw only one harassed waitress. As she galloped by with a tray filled with stacks of pancakes and sausage links, I asked, "Where's Melvinna?"

She stopped at a table and slapped the plates down in front of a couple of men. "You find her, and we'll both know."

"Is she scheduled to work?"

"Yes. Every day but Mondays."

The waitress flew by me. I followed in her wake. "Have you called her?"

"That bozo she lives with doesn't have a phone."

"Hodges?"

She grabbed two pots of coffee with one hand and balanced a tray of mugs on her other. "Who else? The original sugar bear, to hear Melvinna tell it. I wouldn't give the fat slob the time of day."

"Where's he live?" I asked, thinking this would be a good excuse to nose around. "I might swing by and see if she's overslept."

"Out at the end of Wharton Street. Edge of town. Gray trailer. Rents it. They want me to take it over, but I won't step foot in the door until it's been fumigated."

She swept past me but called over her shoulder, "If you see Melvinna, tell her I'm up to my ass in customers. I need help." As she poured a round of coffee, she looked at me hopefully. I escaped before she could voice the query I'd seen in her eyes.

Wharton was four blocks north of Main. I hadn't asked for a house number. I didn't figure I'd need it. I drove out a pockmarked road, passed several houses, then drove for about a quarter of a mile before I spotted Leray's green van. I parked beside it.

The trailer had seen better days. The gray metal skirting was curled up from the foundation. The dark roof had rusted, streaking the sides like mournful brown tears. The yard was mowed, the front stoop free of debris.

I walked down a gravel path to the door and

knocked. Inside, I heard the muted sounds of a television. I knocked harder. When no one came to the door, I tried the knob. It clicked free and swung open.

I put my face to the crack and called, "Bubbles. It's Bretta. You here?"

Nothing but an early morning talk show host expounding on the virtues of fresh fruits as opposed to canned.

"Hello! Anyone home?"

I wrinkled my nose at the odor—overcooked food and something sour and sharp. I leaned in and craned my neck. Living room—shabby; red and black shag carpet, the kind you have to fluff with a rake. No rake had been used on this floor in years. I turned my attention to the other direction—a kitchen table; peeling paint on the ceiling; and a hand on the floor.

I did a double take, then slowly stepped inside.

Hodges was attached to the hand. He lay in the middle of the kitchen floor, still dressed in the same clothes I'd seen him in on Sunday. I didn't need to touch him to know that he was dead. His head was in a dried puddle of vomit; his mouth gaped. His sightless eyes stared at me.

I averted my gaze when my stomach gurgled in rebellion. I stretched the neck of my blouse over my nose and took a quick breath.

The table had been set for two, the plates used. A scum of residue crusted the bottom of the glasses. A mountain of pans teetered on the counter. A greasy skillet sat on the stove. On tiptoe, I peered across the room

163

at the sink, which contained dried and shriveled peel-ings. The rag rug in front of the sink was kicked up, a chair overturned. Black scuff marks from the heels of his boots marred the gold linoleum floor.

A piece of paper was near Hodges's hand. I inhaled deeply of my scent and leaned over. The letterhead read: *Barker Brothers, Inc., Marketville, Ohio.* The contents of Hodges's stomach had blurred parts of the wording, but the gist of the letter was that Barker Brothers would be very much interested in Mr. Hodges's mutation. He was urged to contact them again when he had several blooming specimens.

I quickly reread it, trying to commit the words to memory. I was almost finished when I heard a moan from the back of the trailer.

I'd forgotten Bubbles.

"Bubbles?" I called. Another moan.

I hurried out of the kitchen and was almost through the living room when I saw the empty cage. It was five feet long and made of Plexiglas. The screened top was hinged. The floor of the cage was covered with a scrap of carpet.

Was this Arnie's home? I looked around uneasily. Did Leray have other snakes?

"Help . . . me."

I turned from the cage and walked cautiously down the hall to a room with a decor that was a fat woman's worst nightmare. Even this former fat woman cringed.

Mirrors—hundreds of silver-backed pieces of glass

that never hid the truth. The walls and the ceiling were covered with reflective tiles. It was a slipshod job. The mirrors ran uphill in places. Some didn't match; others were chipped or cracked.

An elaborate chandelier hung from the low ceiling. The dozens of lighted bulbs seemed to make the room vibrate as the mirrors picked up the illumination and tossed them back into my eyes. Black velvet drapes covered the windows. The water bed was a tangle of twisted emerald satin sheets and a leopard skin spread.

Bubbles was sprawled on the floor. She was dressed in a black negligée shot with gold threads. She looked like a bumblebee that had been swatted. I knelt at her side. Her eyes were open, her skin gray.

I quickly assured her that she was going to be fine, and that I would go for help.

In a hoarse voice, she said, "Water." When I hesitated, she pleaded, "Please."

I wasn't sure if it was the right thing to do, but I stepped across the hall into the bathroom. Dried vomit ringed the toilet and had splattered the walls like colorful confetti. I did the number again with my nose under the neck of my blouse. It was the only way I could stand the odor.

I ran an inch of water into a glass I found on the sink. In the bedroom, I carefully raised her head. She drank some, dribbled most of it. When the water ran down her bare skin, she shivered. I covered her with the leopard spread, then got a washcloth from a stack on the toilet tank. I ran cold water on it, squeezed out the excess. When I applied it to her forehead, she stirred weakly.

"I'll go phone for an ambulance," I said.

"No!" She made a grab at my arm, but her fingers didn't have any strength. "Stay. Scared. Arnie loose."

"The snake?"

"Hates me." She swallowed awkwardly, then went limp. I thought she was dead. I felt for a pulse and found a weak beat. I wanted to tell her Arnie was the least of her worries, but she was unconscious.

In my car, I wasted precious seconds trying to decide where to go to call. Not the library. Not the café with all the gossipy coffee drinkers. I finally settled on the funeral home. It wasn't far. I headed for it.

A few minutes later, I pulled up in front of the chapel. I jumped out and ran up the front walk. An old woman in the yard next door stopped what she was doing to give me a strange stare. I guess she'd never seen anyone go eagerly through these doors.

One car was parked in front. On the side drive, the black hearse sat like a giant vulture waiting for its next victim. I assumed it was there for a funeral, but that it was too early for the service.

I jerked open the front door, hurried down the hall, and surprised Margaret in her office. She took one look at my face and whispered, "I have a family here. What's wrong?"

"I need a phone."

She nodded to her desk. I didn't offer explanations.

I dialed 911 and stated what I'd found at Hodges's trailer. A man dead. A woman unconscious.

There were questions, but I had few answers. After I'd said, "I don't know," several times, I ended the conversation with "I'll wait at the trailer," and hung up.

"What are you doing in Woodgrove, anyway?" Margaret asked.

"I had a few loose ends to tie up."

"Loose ends? Was finding Hodges's body one of them?"

"No." I chuckled weakly. "That was an added bonus."

Margaret pursed her lips. "It seems to me—"

"Not now," I said, brushing past her. I wasn't in the mood for any more of her pop psychology. "I have to go back to the trailer. When I left, Bubbles was alive."

Margaret followed me to the door. "Bubbles?"

"Melvinna from the café. We called her Bubbles in high school. Hodges fixed a regular feast. It turned out to be his last supper."

A man and a woman stood in the corridor outside the slumber room where Myrtle Rankin rested peacefully. The woman was wiping her red-rimmed eyes. The man's arm was draped around her waist.

Margaret turned her attention to them with a sympathetic smile. As I hurried away, I heard her say, "Memories of your mother will sustain you in the difficult times ahead. Take comfort that she is with our Lord."

As I got back in my car, a speck of something clogged the wheels of my brain. I hesitated, tried to get the machinery in motion again. Whatever it was, it was gone. And so was I.

Chapter Fifteen

I'd told Lois I'd be back to the flower shop by noon, and I almost made it. It was just after one before I pulled into the alley. My throat was dry from talking, my brain scrambled from a multitude of questions fired at me.

Hodges had been taken to the River City morgue. Bubbles was in River City Memorial Hospital, her chances for recovery good. Sid had raised Cain with everyone. Surprisingly, I'd come through the inferno of his blistering attack merely singed around the edges.

I climbed from the car but only made it as far as the loading dock before my knees began to wobble. I sat down and leaned my head against a wooden post. I gave serious thought to butting it a couple of times. Maybe I could knock some sense into it. My head, not the post, though at this point, one was about as thick as the other.

I wanted to tell Sid about Isaac's plants, but *the sheriff* hadn't been in the mood to listen to any of my what-ifs.

What if . . . Isaac had been propagating a mutation?

What if . . . the plant was worth a bundle of money?

What if . . . a car had been parked behind Sam's property?

What if . . . those boys had swerved to miss it?

What if . . . I didn't know what the hell I was talking about?

Sid thought Hodges had been murdered and was ready to conduct the investigation in that direction. The county coroner, Walter Porter, thought otherwise. On the surface, it looked to him as if Leray Hodges had died by misadventure and damned fool ignorance.

Walt, an old country boy, had taken one look at the peelings and dried leaves in the sink and declared the "parsnips" Hodges had cooked hadn't been parsnips at all. The coroner surmised that Hodges had eaten water hemlock, a plant that grows wild along Missouri ditches and waterways. Its white roots resemble parsnips, even taste like them, but they're deadly when ingested.

The coroner felt that Hodges had simply made a mistake. That's when Sid had gone ballistic. He roared at his men to look long and hard for proof that this was foul play. His men, under the gun, so to speak, had torn the trailer apart. A young deputy had found a wadded-up sack in the trash. To his credit, he'd opened the bag and found a typewritten note inside. I'd gotten a brief glimpse of it before it was tucked away as evidence. It read:

Here's the parsnips from my garden. Enjoy.

No name was signed. Sid had jumped on that note like a duck on a June bug.

Two deaths: Isaac and Hodges. It wasn't any wonder Sid had lashed out at everyone. *Five* murders if you counted those boys. I hadn't dared voice that theory.

The killer had knowledge of water hemlock. Knowledge of Sam's place. Knowledge of Hodges's snake. Knowledge that I was asking questions. Knowledge of the surrounding countryside.

In my ear, I heard Carl's voice. "Obvious, old girl."

But I still didn't see it.

The door creaked open behind me. I looked around and saw Lois hesitate on the threshold. Her shapely eyebrows arched inquiringly.

"Hi," I said.

"Saw you pull in. Kept waiting for you to come inside. When you didn't, I thought I'd better check on you."

I stood up and flipped the dust off the back of my skirt. "I'm okay." I grimaced. "Or as okay as anyone can be who's discovered a body."

Her jaw went slack, then she declared, "You've got to get a new hobby, woman. If you want bodies, try a live one."

Smiling, I followed her into the back room. A shipment of fresh flowers had arrived. She'd been cutting the stems and putting them in water. I grabbed a pair of nippers and picked up a bundle of carnations.

"Been busy?" I asked, stripping away the foliage that would be below the waterline in the bucket.

"Nothing I can't handle."

We worked in silence. Suddenly, Lois gave a disgusted snort. "Well," she demanded, "are you going to tell me whose body?"

"Leray Hodges."

She squinted. "Rings a bell, but I can't place it."

"The guy who trucked Isaac's flowers to Moth."

"Hmm," she murmured. "Plot thickens."

"Like a bowl of week-old gravy."

"So. Tell me."

It was an invitation I could've ignored, but with Lois I didn't have to hedge. While we cut flowers, I laid it all out and added my two cents worth of deciphering the facts. I'd gotten to the part about mutations when the delivery van backed into its customary spot at the loading dock.

"Damn," Lois said. "It's Lew."

"Don't say anything," I whispered as the door opened and Lew Mouffit sauntered into the room.

Lew's a charmer to the customers, but a royal pain to the rest of us. At thirty-eight, he has a fringe of black hair around his shiny bald head. He's never been married, lives with his mother, and he knows something about everything. His main goal in life is to educate us lesser beings.

There are times when I'd like to replace him, but Lew knows this town and its people. He's meticulous in handling the bouquets. The real plus comes when we're busy. He can tie a florist bow swiftly and expertly.

"Hi, boss," he said. "Glad to see you back. Morning deliveries are done." He leaned against the door and watched us work. His eyes followed my movements.

I knew that look. He was about to offer advice.

"You women are a strange breed," he said.

I glanced at Lois, who crossed her eyes. I hid a smile and played along. "How's that?" I asked.

"You go at everything back assward." He pointed to the box of flowers. "You keep reaching around each other to get another bunch of flowers. Wasted motion. Then you walk to the sink and fill *one* bucket. Again, wasted motion. You need to be more efficient. Fill several buckets. Put the flowers within easy reach of you both."

"Why don't you fill the buckets for us?" suggested Lois. "Then we'll get done even more efficiently."

He shrugged and went to the sink. When he'd turned the water on, Lois said, "He's the most irritating man. He knows the easiest, the best way to do anything. I bet he even knows how to pass gas more proficiently."

I shook my head at her, then turned and thanked Lew for the bucket. I plunged liatris, snapdragons, and delphiniums into the warm water.

"Should you put all those flowers in the same..." began Lew, but seeing the gleam in my eye, he stopped, cleared his throat and jovially stated, "Well...so... you're back from Amish country?"

Obviously. I bowed my head over the flowers and said, "Woodgrove isn't exactly—"

He interrupted to pontificate. "Take the Amish—"

"Buggy or car," murmured Lois.

Lew ignored her and continued, "a unique sector of our society. People think of them as freeloaders, but the

173

Amish pay taxes and don't take Social Security or a welfare check. They're a gigantic family who look after each other."

We didn't comment. Lack of audience participation didn't stop Lew. It usually made him try harder.

"Bundling has gone out of style. Too bad. I thought it a very useful custom." He caught our blank stares. In a condescending tone, he explained, "With the consent of the parents, a courting couple would go to bed to get to know each other better."

Sex. A topic to delight two lascivious women. Lew had us, and he knew it. He elaborated. "A folded quilt would be laid between the couples. No serious hanky-panky. Just a bit of touchy-feely and conversation across the bundle. Hence the term, 'bundling.'"

"A different form of birth control," I said.

Lois mused, "I wonder if a folded quilt in the back of a fifty-seven Chevy would have made a difference in my life?"

"Very funny," said Lew. "I suppose you find shunning to be a real kick?"

Lois answered with a retort. I was busy trying to figure out her age. A fifty-seven Chevy. Chad, her oldest son, was . . . Then Lew's words registered through my calculations.

I interrupted him to ask, "Shunning or stunning?"

He gave me a haughty stare. "I said *shunning*."

Edna had told me she thought the person arguing with Isaac had said "stunning," but what if she'd misunderstood? What if it were "shunning"?

Lew was saying, ". . . shunning should have gone by the wayside with bundling. At least with bundling, no one is hurt."

Lois said, "You make it sound evil."

Before Lew could speak, I said, "From what I understand, it can be. Shunning is a form of punishment the Amish practice when a member of their group doesn't conform to the rules of the district. The offender is ostracized by his own people."

"And they still do that?" asked Lois.

Lew, not to be outdone, said, "I'm sure they do. It's a very horrifying fate to be shunned by your family and friends. Imagine what it would be like to be ignored day in and day out by the people you hold most dear. The long-range effects are psychologically inconceivable."

The serious lecture tone disappeared from Lew's voice. "Well," he said, "I had too many deliveries to take a lunch break. I'll be back in an hour."

He left. Lois went up front to wait on a customer. I was rooted to the spot. I must have looked odd—my elbows askew, the nippers in one hand, a bunch of stargazer lilies in the other.

Mentally, I gave myself a boot in the butt. Why hadn't I caught the similarity in the words?

Stunning. Shunning.

Thoughtfully, I mouthed the words. I tried them aloud. Had Isaac been threatened with shunning? Only an Amish person would use that as an inducement to stop growing the flowers.

Bishop Detweiler?

Evan?

Cleome?

Or, what if . . . it was Rosalie?

Slowly, I put the flowers in water and laid the clippers aside. No. Was it possible? Was this the obvious?

I didn't want this to be the answer. Who had the most to lose, outside of Isaac, if he were shunned? His wife. His family. Their entire way of life would be blown to pieces.

"Bretta?" called Lois. "Dan Parker is on the phone. He wants to know if you have a plant order for him."

Reluctantly, I switched gears. "Have you made a list?"

"Yeah. *I* knew he'd be calling today."

I took her light reprimand without comment. I had it coming. "Go ahead," I directed. "Give him your order."

Dan Parker—owner of a large commercial greenhouse on the outskirts of town. Grows huge numbers of wholesale potted plants. Good friend. Grows chrysanthemums.

"Wait!" I shouted. I needed information. Dan Parker was a professional grower. "I want to talk to him."

Frowning, Lois plunked the receiver on the table. "The list is by the phone," she said. "I'll finish the flowers."

"No, stay. I want you to hear this." I called him.

"Dan," I said, "Bretta here. Lois will give you the plant order. But first, I want to ask you something."

"Shoot," he said.

"It's about plant mutations."

"Oh?"

"Do you know what I mean?" I asked, then had to hold the phone away from my ear as he let me know what a dumb question that had been. "Okay, okay." I sighed. "So you know about mutations. What would you do if you found one?"

"I'd develop it. Take cuttings. Watch it. Chart its growth."

Isaac had been following all those steps. "What next?"

"What kind of plant is it?"

I wanted information, I didn't want to give it. "Does that matter?"

His sigh of exasperation whistled in my ear. "Yes, Bretta. It matters."

Reluctantly, I said, "A chrysanthemum."

"Then I'd call my Barker representative."

I made a grab for the worktable to steady myself. "Barker?" The name was difficult to say around the lump of excitement that swelled in my throat.

"That's right. That company's one of the biggest mum developers in the United States."

"Could I call your man myself?"

"I guess so." I heard papers rustle. "Here's his number." He rattled it off. I wrote it down. "Call him after eight in the evening," advised Dan. "That's your best bet in reaching him."

"How much would a mutation be worth?"

"Depends on how unusual. How true the strain is."

This was getting into a sticky area. But if I didn't ask the question, I wouldn't know if I was on to something. "What if it's red?" I inquired softly.

"Red as in burgundy?"

"No," I said. I thought of Isaac's murder. Of the death blow to his skull. I gulped and whispered, "Red, Dan, red, as in . . . blood red."

Out of the corner of my eye, I saw Lois's head swivel toward me. In my ear, Dan was skeptical. "If you've found a red chrysanthemum, Bretta, you won't ever have to work again. But I find it hard to believe. Breeders have tried for years to develop a mum with a Christmas red blossom. The closest they've come is a strain called Bravo, but even then it's more of a deep, dark ruby than the clear red—blood red—you've described." He paused a moment, then asked, "Have you seen it?"

"Almost."

"What's that mean?"

"It's in bud stage, not full bloom. But there was enough color so I'm almost sure."

Casually, Dan asked, "Who has it? Where is this red mutation?"

A note in his voice alerted me. The hairs on my arms stood at attention. At the base of my throat, my pulse beat an erratic rhythm. Dan was trying to suppress his excitement, but I heard it. Too late I realized that if this red chrysanthemum was the motive for Isaac's murder, maybe I shouldn't be blabbing about it.

I tried to be cagey. "I can't say. Right now it isn't mine to show."

"Isn't yours?" He paused, and the businessman in him came across loud and clear. "Are you buying it?"

I'd given him the wrong impression. I opened my mouth to clarify, then stopped. Dan dealt with all the florists and with Moth. If I left Dan wondering, he might try to gain information. His questions asked of the right party might prod someone into action.

Fervently, because my life could depend on the outcome, I said, "I'm investing everything I've got in this deal." I handed the phone to Lois, who took it with a stunned expression.

"It's me, Dan," she said. "I have the plant list. No. I don't know anything about what Bretta said. No, I don't know where it is. No. No. No." She listened for a minute, then snapped, "Do you want this order or not?"

I left her to handle Dan, went to the back, and grabbed the nippers. All day my mind had been engaged in a bunch of what-ifs. Like a favorite song, I replayed them again and again. Only this time I added three more heart-stopping choruses.

What if . . . the killer found out I knew about the red mutation?

What if . . . the killer struck again?

What if . . . the next victim was me?

Chapter Sixteen

In between the telephone orders, customers, and Lew's comings and goings, Lois and I talked over the murders and my theories. By the time five o'clock rolled around, the shop was neat and clean, I'd made a dent in the paperwork on my desk, and Lois had decided I was certifiably insane.

Not bad for a day that had included doing research at the library, finding a corpse, and being interrogated by a sheriff.

I locked up the shop, stopped at the grocery store to stock up on diet munchies, and went home. I put a small steak in a nonstick skillet and added slices of onion, celery, and green pepper to simmer in the natural juices. While a potato baked, I went out on the porch for my paper. It wasn't there.

"Hide-and-seek," I murmured, scanning the yard. "Just what I wanted to do this evening."

I walked down the steps. My gaze circled the ground, the roof of the house, to the ground again, and finally settled on a decorative tree I'd bought with money I'd received from Carl's memorial fund.

Instead of standing tall, the young tree looked ready to topple over from the weight of the newspaper wedged in its branches. "Damn it," I muttered, my heels stabbing the grass as I stomped across the yard.

The tree was only as big around as a nickel, and tonight it was a pitiful sight. It looked like a peasant curtsying before royalty.

Carefully, I worked the paper free. Without the added weight, the sapling sprang upright, but the tender bark had been skinned.

In the house, I tossed the paper on the table, turned the heat down under my steak, and looked up Jamie Fenton's number. I dialed and tried to bring my temper under control.

A man answered.

"Is this the home of Jamie Fenton?" I asked crisply.

"Yes, it is."

"I'd like to speak to him."

"Uh, ma'am. There must be some mistake. Jamie—"

I quickly interrupted. "Are you his father?"

"Well . . . I am Jamie's father, but you see Jamie is—"

"Look. This is Bretta Solomon over on Market Drive. He delivers my papers and, well . . . I'd like to have a word with him."

"Ma'am," he said sharply, "if you'd let me speak, I'm sure we can get to the bottom of this."

"I'm at the bottom. There's nothing left but for Jamie and me to have a talk. I could go to the newspaper office, but I won't do that unless I'm forced to."

His voice was cold. "Name a time."

"Now. Tonight," I said.

"Homework comes first around here."

"This isn't a social call."

"I understand that from your tone."

"I want this foolishness to stop."

"I don't know what you're talking about, but I'll have Jamie call you."

"No. I want to see him face to face."

Suddenly, Mr. Fenton laughed. "That might be a problem if you want to see *him*."

I was so angry, I was shaking. It's parents like him who raise juvenile delinquents. He thought everything was a joke. "You talk to your son," I replied in a tight voice. "See if he'll explain what he's been doing with my paper. I'll leave this matter in your hands." My tone implied that I thought this was a foolish gesture on my part. "If the incidents are repeated," I warned, "I'll be forced to take care of it on my own, and frankly, I don't think you or your son will like the results."

I hung up before Mr. Fenton could speak. "The nerve," I exclaimed. "He's probably known all along what his son's been doing."

I grabbed a bowl out of the cabinet and tore up lettuce for a salad. I snatched and grabbed, rattled pans and silverware. My anger was slow to subside.

That tree was special to me. The money had come from Carl's fellow deputies. I wanted it to live, to thrive. I'd had nurserymen out two or three times to check on its progress. They'd said I'd planted the tree too close to the old cottonwood. The bigger tree was sapping all the moisture and nutrients out of the soil. I was planning to transplant the tree in the backyard this spring where nothing would interfere with its growth.

The timer went off. The potato was done. I gave the steak a gentle poke. It was tender. I turned off the heat and went to my room to slip out of my clothes. I wanted to eat in comfort. Pantyhose and heels didn't fit the bill.

Wrapped in my robe, I was on my way back to the kitchen when the doorbell rang. I didn't try to stifle my annoyance. I was tired, hungry, and not in the mood for company. Without thinking, I flung open the door. I suppose it's not a very smart thing to do when you're up to your eyeballs in a murder investigation.

I was in luck this time. No killer. Just a man and a girl. After I saw the man's expression, I was ready to revise my first thought regarding my safety. He was handsome, or would have been if his face hadn't been scrunched up in a frown. His eyebrows were drawn together, his full lips pressed in a grim line. I looked from him to the girl. She was cute. Short auburn hair, round chubby face, a few freckles scattered like fairy dust across the bridge of her pert nose.

I grinned at her. "Girl Scout cookies, I bet." I shrugged. "I shouldn't buy any, but I can take them to work. Give me a couple of boxes. It doesn't matter what kind."

"No cookies," snapped the man. "I'm Mr. Fenton."

"You are?" I murmured, blinking at him in surprise. "That was fast." I looked past him. "Where's Jamie? I'd rather talk to him."

"That's impossible," he said. "I tried to explain that to you on the phone, but you kept interrupting." He enunciated each word. "*Mrs. Solomon, there is no him.*" He pushed the girl toward me. "Meet Jamie Fenton. My daughter. She delivers your papers."

"Why . . . I . . . uh . . ." I swallowed and forced myself not to stammer. "Come in," I invited. "You've taken me totally by surprise. I had no idea that Jamie was— is a girl."

They stepped into my house, but the man refused to come any further. I closed the door and tried to collect my thoughts. I looked down at Jamie. So she was the plump figure I'd seen riding the bike.

"You're how old?" I asked.

"She's twelve. Will be thirteen next week," replied her father.

"Do you know what this is about?"

"No. Jamie has been extremely silent on the subject."

"Does her mother know?"

His lips hardened. "My wife died three years ago."

"Oh." I looked back at Jamie, who had yet to meet my eyes. "Almost a teenager, huh? Tough age."

She didn't move.

Discovering that Jamie was a girl had taken the wind out of my sails, and even had me fairly embarrassed. I'd never dreamed that a girl was responsible for the tricks played with my newspaper. Briskly, I said, "I was getting ready to eat dinner."

When the father started to speak, I gave him a cutting look. He retaliated with a frown. I ignored him and took Jamie's arm and said, "Come into the kitchen and have a seat. We can talk there."

She spoke for the first time. "I'm not eating."

"But you can keep me company while I eat." I firmly increased the pressure on her arm.

Sullen, she dragged her feet across the room, then slumped in a kitchen chair. Mr. Fenton stood in the doorway. I mulled over the situation while I poured three glasses of iced tea. I handed them around, then dished up my supper.

For the first time, I saw interest on Jamie's face. She watched every move I made. I put the steak on my plate and arranged the bits of steamed vegetables across the top. While I was splitting the potato, a thought occurred. Out of the corner of my eye, I studied her thick arms and double chin, her pudgy body dressed in jogging pants and oversized T-shirt.

Matter-of-factly, I explained, "I don't keep butter in the house. I eat my baked potato with salsa or fat-free ranch dressing." I shrugged. "At first, I missed the buttery flavor, but now, I don't think about it." It was a stretched point that should have twanged like a rubber band. But in this case, I thought it necessary.

I waited. Jamie didn't say anything. Her father, however, was ready with a comment. Before he could speak,

I turned my back to Jamie and jerked a finger across my neck. He got my point and reared back like I'd taken a punch at him. So he'd know I wasn't completely without manners, I tacked on a silent "please" and nodded toward the living room.

He got my message, but he wasn't happy. He mumbled something about waiting in the other room. I took the lid off the salsa jar.

"Hot and spicy. It gives a simple baked potato a Mexican tang." I put half the potato on a saucer, topped it with salsa, added a fork, and slid it across the table to Jamie. "Try it. I lost a hundred pounds eating that."

When she didn't pick up the fork, I turned my attention to the steak. I cut off a bite and put it in my mouth. "Mmm," I said. "Not bad."

She looked at me with wide blue eyes. "Don't you get hungry?"

"Sometimes, but there's always something I can eat. Losing weight has to do with making the right choices."

Jamie picked up the fork and speared a bite of potato. She stared at it. "You're old," she mumbled, then ducked her head. "I mean, it's different for you. I'm with kids who eat cheeseburgers, pizza, and fries all the time. Why don't they get fat? Why just me?"

"I used to feel that way, too. When I was your age, I was the biggest girl in my class. When I got older, I was usually the biggest woman in the room. But my life went on. It was tough. Sometimes I'd cry. Most of the time I just kept eating."

She sighed. "Me, too." She put the bite of potato in

her mouth and chewed. Glancing at the door, she swallowed and lowered her voice. "Dad doesn't help. He works all day, then stops at a fast-food place and picks up dinner. I'm starved when I get off my paper route, and I eat everything."

"Yeah," I agreed. "It's a bad deal."

We ate and chewed in silence. After a while, I asked, "So, why do you keep putting my paper everywhere but on the porch?"

Jamie directed her explanation to her glass of iced tea. "When I took over this route, you were just like Mrs. Sherman down the street."

My fork clattered on my plate. "But Mrs. Sherman is huge."

Jamie shrugged. "You used to be. Now your clothes are loose." Her tone turned accusing. "I've even seen you with your blouse tucked into your slacks. It's not fair," she said. "Every time I see you, you're getting littler and littler, and I'm getting bigger and bigger." She scooped the rest of the potato onto her fork and crammed it in her mouth.

I pushed my plate aside and leaned my elbows against the table. "Let me get this straight. Because I've lost weight and you haven't, you've been doing a number on me with the newspaper?"

She squirmed. "Sounds dumb when you put it that way."

"It *is* dumb."

Jamie eyed my steak. "Are you gonna eat that?"

"Have you had supper?"

"No . . . well, yeah. Dad brought home pizza. But I only had three slices. Then you called."

I rolled my eyes. "Listen, kid, we've got to talk."

"About the paper?"

"Among other things." I raised my voice and called, "Mr. Fenton, could you come in here?"

Jamie's eyes widened in protest. Her young mouth formed a round O of horror. "Not my dad," she whispered fiercely.

"Yes. Your father is part of your problem."

I motioned for Mr. Fenton to have a chair, then I started a pot of coffee brewing. From a shelf in the living room, I pulled a number of books into my arms. Carefully, I stacked them on the kitchen table.

My steady gaze encountered a scowl on Mr. Fenton's face, a blush on Jamie's. "This really isn't any of my business," I began, "but that hasn't stopped me before."

"I heard you say I was part of the problem," said Mr. Fenton. "What problem are we talking about?"

"Jamie's weight," I said.

"Weight!" he groused. "I thought this had to do with your newspaper." He leveled a glare at me. "My daughter is my business. She's a sweet, wonderful girl. She might be . . . uh . . . heavy now, but that's baby fat. She'll grow out of it."

I sat at the table. "Baby fat turns to adult fat. She wants to lose weight. You're the biggest influence in her life." I smiled. "For now, anyway. In a few years, that will change. She needs your help. Are you willing to give it?"

He turned his attention from me to Jamie. "I guess," he mumbled. "I don't know what I can do when I don't see the problem."

"Dad," wailed Jamie, "it's all that junk food you bring home."

"But I thought you loved it."

"I do," she said, "but it doesn't love me. I eat too much. I don't want to be fat. I want to be like the other kids."

Resigned, but not completely convinced, Mr. Fenton said to me, "So you're the guru of food, Mrs. Solomon?"

For a second, a smile flickered at the corner of his mouth. Oh, dear, I thought, he's got dimples. Deep, irresistible dimples.

I tried not to stare as he drawled, "Solomon was very wise." He leaned back in his chair and crossed his arms. "Go ahead," he said. "Let's hear the wisdom of Solomon."

An hour later, they left with the armload of books. As I closed the door, I heard Jamie's bubbling laughter. Her youthful enthusiasm brought a smile to my lips. But it was Mr. Fenton's—Bill's—warm good night that made my heart's rhythm pick up its beat.

I put the kitchen back in order and locked all the doors. After I showered, I lay in my single bed, staring up at the ceiling. Lois says woman was made for man. After Carl died, I figured I'd had my chance. I'd lived it. I'd loved it. I'd lost it. Bill hadn't said anything about calling me. He hadn't given me any indication that he wanted to see me again. But the warmth in his brown eyes had thawed a part of me that I'd thought had died with Carl.

Before I switched off the light, I turned on my side and faced the hallway. A corner of the master suite door was visible. My bed was narrow and lonely. The bed in the suite was king-size but just as desolate. I hadn't been in that room since Carl died. Approximately four hundred and fifty-six nights of being alone. A tear trickled from my eye and onto the pillow.

The brain is ruled by a strange and miraculous science. It can be fine-tuned to the point that minor incidents from the past can be recalled. On the other hand, that same globe of gray matter can masterfully conceal details that bring pain.

I turned off the lamp and stretched out. When I closed my eyes, I knew the images would be there. I swallowed and let the pictures form. My breathing went from slow to raspy. Each breath was like a knife in my chest.

Carl. Warm and alive. His smile as intimate as a kiss. His thick dark hair tousled. His amber eyes brimming with tenderness and passion.

Passion. I shuddered. It was a killer.

Chapter Seventeen

☀ I awoke the next morning with the uneasy feeling that I'd forgotten something. I poured my coffee and was thinking about breakfast when I saw the note by the phone.

The Barker representative. Calling him had completely slipped my mind. A glance at the clock told me it was too early, but then again, he might be up, getting ready to leave on his route. If I didn't call now, I'd have to wait until eight tonight. I wanted as much information as possible before I talked to Evan after work.

I put the number in front of me and dialed. It was answered by a sleepy male. "Yes?" he mumbled.

"Are you the representative from Barker Brothers?" I asked.

"This is Norton Munsterman."

I almost laughed. Norton? I cleared my throat and said, "My name is Bretta Solomon." Oops! Should I have given him my real name? Too late now. "Uh ... Dan Parker gave me your number. I'm sorry to call so early, but I need some information."

"What about?"

"Mutations. How much would one be worth?"

He didn't answer immediately, but I could hear him breathing. Finally, he said, "Since Dan gave you my number, I'm assuming you're tackling a chrysanthemum mutant."

"That's right."

His tone was guarded. "I'm not authorized to quote sums. I sell cuttings to growers. I help them establish a rotation plan for growing pot mums."

"Generally, then, are they worth money?"

"Are you asking if it's beneficial for a propagator to pursue a sport?"

"Isn't that what I said?"

He chuckled. "In a roundabout way."

"Well, are they?" I persisted.

"Depends on the sport. What are we talking about? Size of blossom? Color? Shape of flower? Growth habit?"

I was getting more questions than answers. "Could we keep this purely hypothetical, Mr.—uh—Munsterman? I don't need a figure. I just want to know if a mutant could be worth money?"

"Hypothetically, sure. A woman back east is a millionaire several times over. One of the lavender mums in her backyard mutated with an unusual number of petals."

"Millions?" I gulped. "From a chrysanthemum?"

"Not just any chrysanthemum, Miss—Mrs.—uh—Sodamen. A sport. A one-of-a-kind that's never been seen before. Barker's doesn't pay that amount in one lump sum. Royalties are paid on each cutting that's sold and shipped out to the growers. In some cases, it's only a few cents a plant, but over a year's production, the sum can be staggering."

I said my thanks, assured him that if the sport proved to be exceptional, I would call him. When I hung up, my stomach was jumping. Millions?

I went to my room to get my purse. When I came to the master suite, I stopped and stared at the wooden panel. I knew the time was coming when I'd have to face that room and all its grievous memories. Last night I'd allowed myself to remember the Carl I'd loved, the Carl who was alive and vibrant. Soon I'd have to explore the circumstances of his death, and my denial in dealing with them. I'd have to put my loving ghost to rest. It was time.

I touched the brass doorknob and drew a sharp, painful breath. I exhaled slowly. But not today.

On the drive to the flower shop, I kept thinking about all the money that could be involved in Isaac's mutations. Wealth was too worldly for the Amish. Isaac wouldn't have been interested. But Hodges, Moth, Sam Kramer, and Cecil were all mercenary men.

Would Bishop Detweiler have allowed Isaac to take the money? Never. If Detweiler disapproved of Isaac selling flowers for profit, the old man would pop his cork if he knew millions were involved. But maybe he already did.

I parked in the alley and tried to pressure myself into

figuring things out. It was a no-go. Around and around my thoughts went. I'd settle on a suspect, then fact would refute it. I'd settle on another, but my heart wasn't into believing people I knew were capable of murder.

For the time being, I gave up and went into the shop. We were kept busy with orders but never rushed. Over the course of the morning, while we worked, I filled Lois in on my conversation with the Barker representative. I cleaned out the back cooler and made several fresh bouquets for the front display case.

Lois and I were too busy to go out for lunch, so we had Lew pick up a pizza. I'd promised myself one slice. To offset the extra calories, I'd have a salad for supper. It was a good plan, but I hadn't counted on my weakness for food overriding my convictions. Like an alcoholic who can't take that first drink, so it goes with someone addicted to food.

I'd eaten two pieces for lunch. It was now after three o'clock. The box was sitting within easy reach. I didn't fight the urge. I grabbed a third wedge.

I was chewing and contemplating a particularly difficult order, when the front doorbell jingled. Lois went up front to wait on the customer. I didn't bother looking up. My attention was on my order. It called for a sweet and dainty bouquet. Fine. I could handle that. I arranged pink carnations, miniature roses, white daisies, and baby's breath in a pastel wicker basket. What had me stymied was how to incorporate the customer's favorite fourteen-inch stuffed elephant into the arrangement.

I had the toy in one hand and the slice of pizza in the other when Lois said, "Bretta, this young lady is here to see you."

I looked up and there stood Jamie at the counter. My first impulse was to ditch the pizza in the trash can under my table. Instead, I put down the elephant and motioned for her to come closer.

When she was at my table, I laid the pizza carefully on a napkin. "I could have tossed that in the trash when I saw you, but you might as well know dieting isn't easy. You'll have days when you want to eat everything in sight. Usually, I fight the urge. Today, I concede this battle, but there's still tomorrow. I haven't lost the war."

Puzzled, Jamie asked, "What made you eat pizza today?"

Before I answered, I pulled a step stool closer, then perched on the seat. At this level I could look directly into Jamie's troubled blue eyes. I hoped I'd find the right words to make her understand.

"Losing weight isn't just about food, sweetheart, it's about emotions, stress," I touched my chest, "stuff going on inside you. I ate pizza today because I have some personal issues that are bothering me. I also ate it because I get tired of worrying and thinking about what I can and can't have."

Jamie ducked her head shyly. "I passed up three cookies and a bag of chips today."

Tears burned my eyes. I gave her pudgy little body a brief hug. "Gosh, that's wonderful. I'm proud of you." I looked at her closely. "How did it make you feel?"

The wide grin that stretched across her face made her freckled little nose wrinkle. "It wasn't so bad. Dad packed me a lunch. Grapes and a sandwich with low-fat turkey and lettuce. Tonight, we're going to the grocery store. He says there's a woman at work who brings chocolate cookies. The kind that don't have very many calories. I can only have two, but that sounds great."

"So your dad is helping out, huh?"

"Big time. He says it won't hurt him to shed a few pounds, too." She took a step back. "I've got to go. My paper route, you know." She shot me a quick look. "Can I come by or ... uh ... call you if I have"—she nodded to the slice of pizza—"one of your kind of days?"

I leaned forward and touched her auburn curls. "You can come see me or call anytime. I'd love to have you and your father over for dinner one night. I can show both of you some of my quick and easy meals."

Jamie nodded thoughtfully. "Yeah. That'd be great. Dad needs a woman in his life—besides me, of course." She waved good-bye and hurried away.

Lois stood looking after her but waited until the door had closed before she turned to me. Her tone was serious. "As a mother of five children, I have to tell you ..."

I cringed, expecting the worst. After all, I didn't have one iota of experience with children.

". . . you did a helluva job, Bretta. You handled her like a pro. You gave her just what she needed." She waggled her eyebrows in a disgustingly lecherous manner. "Now tell me about Dad. How old is he? Have you met him? Is he cute? Best of all, I take it, the man is single."

Before I could answer, the phone rang. Lois made a face. "This topic is far from closed," she warned, as she picked up the receiver.

Being with Jamie had given me a warm, fuzzy feeling. Without an ounce of regret, I dropped the pizza in the trash, then zeroed in on the damned elephant. Suddenly, I smiled. I grabbed a bolt of pink satin ribbon and made a big fluffy bow. I attached it to the elephant's neck and tied the ends of the ribbon to the handle of the basket. The elephant wasn't *in* the arrangement, but he looked like he was smelling the flowers. It was sweet, cute, and *done*. I took the bouquet to the back for Lew to deliver.

By four, the phones had stopped ringing. All the orders were finished, and I'd answered as many of Lois's questions about Bill Fenton as I could.

"I think I'll go on over to Evan's," I said to Lois.

"Are you going to tell him that Isaac's mums could be worth big bucks?"

"I don't know. He's already decided to get rid of Isaac's field flowers. He may plan on disposing of the greenhouse plants, too."

Lois gasped in horror. "What if he already has?"

"I don't think so, unless Detweiler's harping convinces him. When I was there Sunday, the plants had been freshly watered. I think he'll look after them for a while. But I can't put off talking to him."

"Go," said Lois, waving me impatiently on my way. "It makes me crazy to think something worth a fortune is just sitting there in a dishpan."

I arrived at Evan's house forty-five minutes later. Storm clouds had gathered in the south. The crisp, warm days of September were about to give way to a cold, dreary fall rain. The sound of thunder rumbling in the distance accompanied me up the steps to the back porch. I knocked.

Katie came shyly to the door. "Hi," she said. "We're baking."

I sniffed appreciatively. "I could smell it all the way from River City." She giggled until her mother called from inside.

The humor in Katie's face died. Soberly, she held the door open. "Come in," she said. "I have work to do." She slipped past me. I wanted to touch her, to bring a smile back to her lips, but I couldn't say anything with Cleome sitting there. The Amish woman ruled her brood with a stern hand, and I knew better than to interfere.

I was annoyed with Cleome, but I couldn't help admiring the scene before me. It had all the nostalgia of a Thomas Hart Benton painting. Jars of jelly sat in neat rows on the counter. Two loaves of freshly baked bread rested nearby. Three pies were cooling on the table. Cleome sat in a rocking chair, a stained apron across her lap, her hands busy with a bowl and a paring knife.

She looked almost charming with her devotional cap tied on top of her braided hair. But I knew her tongue could be as razor-edged as the knife in her hand.

My tone was cool. "I came to see Evan."

Cleome matched that temperature. "He's busy."

"I'm sure he is." I leaned against the cabinet and watched the blade slice through the brown skin of a potato. "Where is he?"

She didn't answer. She stood up and went to the sink, where she operated a hand pump. After rinsing the potatoes, she filled a pan with water, cut the potatoes into cubes, and set the pan on the stove. Once the flame had been adjusted to her satisfaction, she stared at me. "Leave us alone," she said.

Direct. I could deal with that. I was a forthright person. "Not yet," I countered.

Cleome pursed her lips and pulled a lethal-looking butcher knife from a drawer. My eyes widened. But she only went to a dishpan where a chicken carcass soaked.

She attacked the bird with the knife, pierced the meat, and exposed the bone. I watched, mesmerized by her nimble fingers. They always seemed to be in danger of a painful nick, but she'd move them out of the way. The chicken pieces would separate and fall into the bloody water.

I waited until she'd finished and had put down the knife. I wanted another go-around with Cleome, but not while she held that dagger in her hands.

Before I could speak, the door opened and Katie came in with a basket of sun-dried clothes. On her way through the kitchen, she said, "Bretta is to stay for supper." Her chin trembled when Cleome turned, but Katie didn't yield ground. However, she did switch from English to their dialect.

It didn't take an Einstein to figure out what was said. The words weren't familiar, but I know a butt-chewing when I hear it, in any language.

Katie's eyes filled with tears. I winked at her and said, "After we eat, I'd like to take a walk. Maybe go down to the creek." Out of the corner of my eye, I saw Cleome frown. Recklessly, I added, "I'm sure your father won't care. I'll fix it with him."

Cleome waited until Katie had left the room, then whispered fiercely, "Take your walk. Enjoy your *last* evening here. It's all behind us now."

"Behind you?" I exclaimed.

"Evan plowed up Isaac's flowers today. He'll sow wheat tomorrow. Hodges is dead. He won't be bothering Rosalie or any of us again."

"He was murdered, Cleome, so it isn't finished. It's your right not to see me again, but don't you want the guilty person punished?"

"Our Lord will take care of that."

"What if the reason for Isaac's murder still exists? What if the killer comes back? He has to be found."

Cleome's lips spread into a pious smile. "It doesn't matter. In our Lord's words, 'When he knoweth of it, then shall he be guilty.' We don't know anything. None of this concerns us. We are not involved. We are not answerable to you, either."

Her calm, condescending attitude was like tossed gas on a smoldering fire. My temper flared. "Soon," I prophesied, "regardless of what you want, the outside world will come knocking on your door."

I'd just finished delivering my bit of prognostication when tires crunched on the drive. Cleome stared at me, then out the window. A burgundy van labeled RIVER CITY WHOLESALE FLORAL CO. had parked behind my car. The van door opened, and J. W. Moth stepped out.

"Company," I murmured. "Not who I'd have predicted."

"Who is that?" demanded Cleome uneasily.

"The buyer of Isaac's flowers."

She relaxed. "Oh. He's too late. They're all gone." With a contented smile, Cleome went back to the stove.

I watched from the kitchen window. Moth surveyed his surroundings. He glanced at my car, looked at the house. The wind ruffled his thinning hair. He tugged at the waistband of his jeans. Jeans? Moth? I snorted. Moth had dressed down for his visit to an Amish farm.

Some men wear denim with ease; it fits their form naturally. I grinned when Moth dug at the seam that rode in his crack. I chuckled softly at his annoyed scowl. He rubbed his hands down his pants legs, tugging at the material bunched at his crotch.

Moth's adjustments came to a halt when he saw Evan

crossing the yard. With mincing steps, he hurried over and said, "Mr. Miller, I had some free time and thought I'd pay you a call."

Evan's voice was low. I didn't catch what he said. Moth's answering voice squeaked. "I know, but I hoped I might get you to change your mind."

Evan shook his head. Behind me, Cleome tittered. The two men had walked out of my line of vision. Moth's voice was muffled. I decided I'd have to go out and hear their conversation firsthand, perhaps interject a comment or two.

I stepped onto the porch and Moth turned. His expression wasn't filled with delight at the sight of me. He nodded curtly, then concentrated again on Evan.

Moth's high-pitched voice deepened with emotion. "This is a tragic situation, Mr. Miller. You've lost a brother, and I've lost a good friend."

What a crock, I thought in disgust. This man's acting abilities were being wasted in Missouri. He should have been onstage somewhere, anywhere but here. I was moved by his performance, moved to the point I wanted to kick his scrawny little butt off Evan's property.

"Would it be possible for me to see Isaac's greenhouse?" Moth asked. "We had some marvelous plans." He sighed forlornly. "Now, I'm at a loss. I assume, as his brother, you'll honor my agreement."

"Agreement?" repeated Evan. "I don't know anything about an agreement." His eyes shifted to me. "Bretta, do you know what he's talking about?"

I pasted a smile on my face. I couldn't tell Moth to

take a flying leap. After all, I did depend on him for the bulk of my cut flowers. I had other options, but Moth was in River City when I needed supplies in a hurry.

"This isn't a good time," I explained. "As for the agreement, that will depend on Isaac's widow. I don't believe she's seeing anyone yet."

It was amusing to watch Moth's face. The total of my monthly flower statement must have flashed before his eyes. He struggled to be gracious, though his first instinct must have been the same as mine regarding him. He swallowed his ill humor and nodded agreeably. "Perhaps in a day or two, I can come back and see the glasshouse. I'll make an offer for its contents."

"Do you have a price in mind?" I asked innocently.

"No" was his short reply. To Evan, he was more congenial. "When I make an offer for Isaac's plants, the sum will be fair." Casually, he asked, "Are they in the greenhouse? Are they being taken care of?"

Evan darted a swift look at me. I met that look and felt a rock settle in my stomach. Oh, boy. Something was wrong. Until I knew the problem, I didn't want Moth privy to any information. Evan started to speak, but I loudly overrode him. I assured Moth that I'd seen the plants and they were in excellent condition.

This news didn't set well. He sniveled, "If she's seen them, why can't I, especially if I'm buying them?"

"I'm a friend of the family. I'm staying for supper. Since you haven't bought anything yet..." My voice trailed away.

Moth clamped his lips together and walked to his van. He climbed up on the seat and started the engine. "I'll be back in a few days," he called in parting.

Evan and I watched Moth maneuver the van out of the driveway and onto the blacktop. Once he was on his way, Evan asked, "What agreement? Isaac never said anything about any agreement."

I gave him a quick rundown on what I'd learned and what I suspected. Someone knew the value of Isaac's red mums, and lots of greedy people had hopes for making money.

"Not anymore," said Evan. "Come see Isaac's plants."

I didn't wait for Evan. I ran across the yard. At the greenhouse door, I paused to look at Isaac's field. The flowers were gone. Plowed under. Here and there were bits of green stems, and a few ragged flower heads waved dejectedly above the freshly turned earth.

I smelled rain in the air. The clouds were closing in on the sun. Tears filled my eyes. It was a sad, desolate picture.

At my side Evan murmured, "I did that today. It was like burying Isaac all over again."

There was nothing to say. I turned to the greenhouse and went down the steps. Shock took my breath away. I stared in amazement. All the plants were dying: shriveled stems; dried-up leaves; buds limp and black.

"What happened, Evan?" I managed to ask. "What did you do?"

"Nothing. They just started dying."

"But I saw them Sunday. They were fine." I walked

down the aisle. "A plant doesn't die this quickly. It doesn't turn black."

I touched a leaf with a fingertip. It fell, setting off a chain reaction. More leaves fell like shattered dreams. "I don't get it," I mumbled. "When did you first notice there was a problem?"

"Yesterday, they didn't look right. This morning they were worse."

I sniffed a few times.

Gruffly, Evan said, "It's nothing to cry over, Bretta."

"I'm not crying. Don't you smell that? What is it?"

He shrugged. "Just greenhouse, I guess."

"No. That isn't greenhouse." I frowned, trying to think. "I've smelled it before." I closed my eyes in concentration. A memory was just at the edge of my mind. I could almost see it, but it didn't look right. It didn't fit my scenario of events. I opened my eyes and found Evan staring at me. He must have thought I'd lost my mind. I asked him, "Did you fertilize the plants?"

"No. I just watered them from the holding tank." Evan pointed. "The tank is buried underground. We use a small pump to push the water through the hose."

"Where do you fill the tank?"

"The spout is outside. The water comes from our main well."

"Pump me some water, Evan. I want to see it."

His shoulders slumped. "Aw, Bretta, that pump is old and needs fixing. Most of the time I have to carry water from the house to prime it."

My jaw was set. Evan sighed. "All right. But can I just dip out a bucket?"

"I don't care how you do it. I want to see the water that's in the storage tank."

"It'll take me a few minutes."

He moved a small potting bench, then slid a piece of sheet metal to one side to reveal a trap door that was two feet square. He flipped it up. I leaned over to look in, but it was too dark to see. He found a piece of rope and tied it to a bucket. Slowly, he lowered it into the hole. We heard the *kerplunk* as it hit bottom.

The odor was stronger over the trap door. It made my nose tingle. "How much water does this storage tank hold?" I asked.

"About three hundred gallons, but there's not that much in here now. I haven't gotten around to filling it."

Evan drew the bucket up and set it down. It contained only about three inches of water, but it was enough to see that it was clear.

Something had been added to the storage tank. Something so deadly it had killed the plants in four days. I walked to the far end of the greenhouse and stared at the dying parent plant. Not a sprig of green anywhere, or I'd have hustled it off for Dan Parker to save.

All of Isaac's painstaking work was gone. He might not have wanted the money, but his widow and children deserved to have this plant. It had been part of Isaac's life. Now it was dead. It had been murdered with the same calculated ruthlessness that had killed him.

Chapter Eighteen

On the walk back to the house, Evan told me the reason for his spontaneous invitation for me to join them for supper. Jacob, Emily, Matthew, and Mark had gone home with the relatives for a visit. Luke and John were too young to care, but Katie had wanted to go with her older siblings. I was her consolation prize. My words, not Evan's.

Our small group was lost at the big trestle table. The meal began with a silent prayer. I'd eaten Cleome's cooking several times in the past. The menus weren't designed for a calorie- or cholesterol-reduction diet. The recipes didn't come from a "time saver" or a "quickie meal planner" article out of a magazine. This was food to sate a workingman's appetite.

I gazed at the banquet before me. Fried chicken, mashed potatoes with cream gravy, and green beans cooked with bits of home-cured ham. There was a plate of biscuits, each crusty, golden sphere more than three inches tall and accompanied by a blue crock of country-churned butter. Dessert was the pies I'd seen earlier.

I gulped. I thought I'd blown my diet eating pizza. What was I going to do now?

As I put some food on my plate, I searched my brain. If my mouth was open talking, I couldn't be shoveling food into it. All I needed was a subject. Something that would be of interest to my Amish listeners.

I looked around me. Mom was gone. An entirely different kind of life was being lived within these walls, but there was the same feeling of love and family here. I smiled as I remembered Mom and me popping corn, then sharing a bowl while we laughed at the antics of Red Skelton on television.

Amish don't have televisions. The farm? Mom and me driving the tractor into the pond. Amish don't use tractors. I looked at the jelly on the counter. I relaxed and talked about something everyone at the table could appreciate.

A kerosene lamp hung from a hook in the ceiling. The glow cast shadows on the planes and hollows of the faces around me. The family's clothes were dark and somber, but their eyes were alight with curiosity.

"My mother was a wonderful woman, but she thought the only reason we had summer was so we could work in the garden. We pickled beets, shucked corn, shelled peas, broke beans." I took a deep breath and added, "We stemmed strawberries, peeled peaches, crushed grapes." I grinned. "By fall my fingers were almost stubs, but the cellar was packed with jars full of preserved fruits and vegetables."

"And you helped?" asked Katie, in awe of this revelation.

I smiled at her. "I think I spent more time in the garden than I did playing at the creek."

"What did you play?"

I waved away Evan's offer of a second helping of chicken. "Well, let's see. I'd take my dolls, Mom would fix me a snack, and I'd have a picnic. You're lucky to have brothers and sisters to play with. When I was your age, it was just me and the birds and frogs. I'd stay as long as Mom would let me."

Katie gave Cleome a shy look. "But it's never long enough."

Embarrassed by their rapt attention, I chuckled. "That was many, many years ago, but I'd still like to see that old tree and the creek." I pushed my plate away and declined Cleome's offer of a piece of pie.

Thunder rumbled. This time it was closer.

"It's going to rain," said Katie fretfully, eyeing the changing weather.

"I like walking in the rain," I replied.

Cleome started to shake her head, but Evan said, "We'll save dessert for later. Go on. A little water never hurt anyone."

We bowed our heads for the silent prayer that ended the meal. Once every head was up, Katie jumped from her chair and hurried to the door.

"Maybe it won't rain until we get back," she said hopefully and pushed open the door to skip down the steps.

I paused long enough to thank Cleome for the meal. Her eyes met mine. I was surprised to see a gleam of respect. Had she and I finally found common ground? I thought of Mom's blue granite canner sitting unused on a shelf in my garage. Impulsively, I offered it to Cleome.

For a moment, I thought she was going to smile. It was there at the corner of her mouth, but she wouldn't let it free. "I can put it to good use" was all she said.

I nodded to her, then glanced at Evan. He gave me a sly wink before picking up a book.

Outside, the sky was crowded with ominous, roiling clouds. The wind had picked up, bringing a freshness of rain already fallen somewhere close by. I caught up with Katie, whose exuberance was a match for the swirling tempest overhead.

From the house, the land sloped gently to the creek. Past the creek was the back pasture where the ground leveled out to the Millers' property fence. Beyond that was the gravel road and the Bellows' acreage.

Daylight had faded, but trees were visible, their leafy branches black against the navy sky. Lightning streaked occasionally, but it wasn't close enough to cause us concern.

Katie had brought a flashlight, but I assured her I didn't need it. Our destination was marked by the oak tree that stood like a friendly giant patiently watching our approach. It was much taller than its companions, its girth more than Katie and I could've reached around. Years had passed since I'd been this way, but the tree was as I'd remembered—the roots exposed, creating neat crevices where we could sit.

For a time, we didn't speak. We listened to the water ripple over the rocks in the creekbed. Off to our left, a bird chirped a warning that strangers were about.

"I like it here," whispered Katie. Her voice was soft and dreamy. "It's a good place to think."

"When I was your age, I'd lie back and stare up at the stars. I'd wonder all sorts of things."

"You would?"

"Yeah. Like what keeps an airplane in the air. Or why you can make bread one time, and it's light and tasty, and the next it isn't fit to feed to a dog."

She laughed. "Or how about, why do the stars just hang? Or what makes clouds so fluffy?"

I pointed. "Those clouds don't look very fluffy to me. We'd better start back. I have to drive home, yet."

Katie sighed. "I don't know why it had to rain to-night."

Before I could reply, I heard voices from across the creek. "That sounds like Cleome."

Katie stirred uneasily. "Yes."

I strained my ears. "Is that Edna with her?"

"Sometimes after supper they meet to visit." She glanced at me. "We're not supposed to tell, or Mr. Bellows will be mad."

I almost snorted. Mad wouldn't begin to describe Cecil's reaction to his wife being friends with an Amish woman.

"Does Evan know?" I asked.

Katie nodded. "We feel sorry for Edna. She doesn't have many friends."

A word popped into my mind. Without thinking, I said it aloud. "Shunning."

Beside me, Katie gasped and came nimbly to her feet. My muscles didn't react nearly as quickly, but I scrambled up. "What is it, Katie?"

She stammered, "Why...uh...what...we don't talk about that."

"It's all right, Katie. I'm sorry, I said—"

"What's wrong with flowers?" she asked.

"What do you mean?"

"Bishop Detweiler said if Isaac went against the council's decision, it would be the same as going against God. Isaac would have to be punished. But I don't understand. All he did was grow flowers."

This was Evan and Cleome's job to explain. Not mine. "Let's go back to the house," I suggested. "Keep the light off. We can find our way."

We stepped from the grove of trees through some tall fescue grass and into the mowed pasture. The rain was fast approaching. I could feel the mist on my face.

We quickened our steps. I was ready to make a dash for cover, when I heard a vehicle on the gravel road. I stopped when it slowed down. Was it Cecil? Had he discovered Edna's secret? I waited for his shout of anger. The car's engine shut off. A door closed.

"Who's that?" asked Katie.

"I don't know. Let's watch." Afraid our silhouettes

might be seen, I tugged on her arm, and we knelt on the pasture.

It was a man. His low oath carried to us, followed by the sound of cloth tearing. We heard a dull thud, then a figure appeared. He held a flashlight, the beam bright. It pinpointed his limping progress across the open field.

"Is that Mr. Bellows?" worried Katie.

"No," I said grimly. "Go to the house and get your father. Tell him to meet me at Isaac's greenhouse."

"If it isn't Mr. Bellows, who is it?"

I had a good idea, but I wanted to catch him in the act. In her ear, I whispered, "Tell Evan to be very quiet and not to have a light on."

Katie trembled. I put my arm around her slim shoulders. "Do as I say. Keep your light off. Circle the pasture so he doesn't see you."

"Is it who killed Isaac?"

I gave her a hug of reassurance. "Go get your father. We'll take care of it."

She hurried off. I trailed the intruder as he loped along. He hunkered close to the ground, but the light remained on.

I worked my way to within sixty feet of him. I wanted to close the distance, but I was afraid he'd turn and flash the light behind him. When he topped the hill near Isaac's field, the light went out.

Had he changed his mind? Or had he scurried on? Taking a chance, I assumed the latter and picked up my pace. When I reached the crest, the clouds split and a deluge of rain bombarded the field. My shirt was soaked in an instant. I stopped long enough to wipe the water from my eyes. Through the plopping of raindrops, I heard the unmistakable sound of an umbrella being swooshed open.

I clenched my teeth and muttered, "Pompous little turd."

We neared the greenhouse. I rubbed my chilled arms and looked longingly at Evan's house. Was he on his way?

The grass was slick under my feet, and my hair straggled in my eyes. A light flashed on briefly as the man got his bearings. I moved faster now that I knew exactly where he was. The greenhouse door creaked open. His shoes crunched on the gravel steps; then he was inside.

I waited to see if Evan was nearby. But I heard only silence and the *pitter-patter* of rain on the glass roof. Would the intruder turn on his light? I waited. His greed won out over his fear of discovery. The light came on, and he drew a sharp breath.

Carefully, I followed him down the steps. He had his hand over the lens to diffuse the glare. From the crook of his arm dangled the collapsed umbrella. I crept closer.

In the glow, his face was pale. His pointed nose emphasized his weasel appearance. His actions deserved my crude assessment. He was a sneak thief. My lips curled with contempt as he played the light over the dying plants.

"All dead," I said quietly. "Just like Isaac."

J. W. Moth whirled. Like a cornered animal, he searched for a means of escape. There was none. I blocked the only exit.

Moth was desperate. He shone the light into my face. Blinded, I instinctively put up a hand. He swung hard and his umbrella slammed into it. I groaned as pain shot up my arm. I couldn't see, but I heard his feet crunch on the gravel as he rushed me. I put both arms up and received another vicious pounding with the damned umbrella. I reached for it but couldn't get a hold.

Moth caught me off balance and pushed me aside. I fell. As he leaped over me, I made a grab for his ankle. I connected, and he sprawled across me. His knee hit my chin, and for a second, I saw stars.

I shook my head to clear my vision and saw the flashlight had fallen on the bench. It was tilted up to the roof. The light reflected on the water-spotted glass overhead, turning the drops into a treasure trove of sparkling gems.

Moth's curse filled the air as he tried to wiggle out of my grasp. I'd hoped he'd lost his "weapon" in the scuffle. No such luck. He countered my attack by beating my hands, my back, and my face with the umbrella.

I let go of his ankle, and he struggled to his feet. He picked up the flashlight but aimed it away from my eyes. Holding the umbrella like a sword, he backed toward the steps.

I came slowly to my feet and inched toward him. My aggressive action infuriated him.

"Stay away from me," he warned.

"You aren't going anywhere," I declared. "If you do, the sheriff will hunt you down."

"Hunt me down?" he whined. "I didn't do anything. I only wanted to see the plants."

"*Murder* isn't anything?"

"Murder?" he squeaked. The umbrella wavered. "What are you talking about?"

"Isaac." The name dropped between us.

The umbrella dipped to the ground. "What does that have to do with me?"

"How did you know to cross the pasture to get here?"

"I saw the road this afternoon when I left the Millers'. I followed it and decided to come back tonight to see the mutation."

"It wasn't the first time you crossed that pasture," I accused. "You did it the same night you killed Isaac."

Moth looked bewildered, but not so addled that he didn't notice I'd worked my way closer. The umbrella came up. He pointed the silver tip at my throat.

"You're crazy," he shouted. "I'm going back to town, and you can't stop me."

"But I can," said Evan. His voice drifted eerily from the shadows. It caught Moth off guard.

Moth swiveled the light in Evan's direction. The Amish man looked impressive in the illumination. Rain had plastered his workshirt to his muscular arms. Moisture dripped from his face and ran in rivulets into his black beard. When the light flashed in his eyes, Evan stood like stone, never wincing.

"Mr.—uh—Miller," stammered Moth, "I—uh—well . . ." Finding an adequate explanation beyond his capabilities, Moth did the only thing he could. He ran. He zipped by Evan and up the steps.

"Why didn't you grab him?" I demanded.

Calmly, Evan stepped farther into the greenhouse. He took a packet of matches from his pocket and lit the lantern in his hand.

I ran up the steps and peered after Moth into the gloom. "Hurry," I called to Evan. "He's getting away."

Evan adjusted the flame, then moved at a snail's pace up to where I stood. He held the lantern above his head, and we saw Moth fleeing across the pasture in a drizzle of rain.

"We have to stop him," I said, and I took a couple of steps. When Evan didn't follow, I turned and asked, "What's wrong?"

"I don't fight."

My nerves were as fragile as wet tissue paper. "I'm not asking you to fight him, Evan. Just detain him until the sheriff can get here."

Stubbornly, Evan shook his head.

"Then give me the damned lantern," I said. "I'll go after him."

"No."

"What?" I screeched. I was wet and angry. I hadn't taken a beating from Moth just so he could climb in his car and drive merrily away.

I don't know how long we would have stood there, Evan impassive, me doing an indignant burn. From up the hill came a harsh exclamation. It was followed by a scream of unadulterated terror.

Moth's light had diminished in the distance. Now we saw it come bobbing back. He slipped and slid down the hill. His cry for help echoed in the night.

"Stop him!" he screamed. "It's the devil himself."

We watched in amazement as Moth sprinted toward us. Beside me, Evan began to chuckle. At first, it was a low, hollow sound deep within his throat. Finally, it burst from his mouth in great belly laughs. I thought he'd gone nuts.

I strained to see the humor. Slowly, a smile of satisfaction spread across my face. Saul, the wayward goat, had come to the Millers' for a bedtime snack. It was Moth's misfortune that he'd crossed paths with the goat: Moth's instinct was to run. Saul's was to give chase.

I wasn't as amused as Evan, but I felt that my beating was about to be vindicated. Moth begged for us to rescue him. When we did nothing, his steps faltered. This was the opening the goat needed.

Saul lowered his head. He put on a fresh burst of speed. I saw it coming. I flinched as the horns dug into Moth's soft posterior. Right on target. Moth stumbled, hit a patch of mud, and sprawled at our feet.

"Touchdown," I said. "Score one for our side."

Chapter Nineteen

My enthusiasm at seeing Moth bested lasted about as long as the storm. The clouds had already shuffled off to reveal a pale, watery moon. Biting my lip, I put my hand out to Moth in a gesture of reconciliation.

He looked at it, then said, "You accused me of murder."

I retaliated. "You beat me with your umbrella and trespassed on Evan's land."

Moth nodded once. "So I did." He put his hand in mine, and I jerked him to his feet. He was a pitiful figure, but he wasn't the killer. Now that I had the chance to think calmly about it, his amazement at my accusation had had the ring of truth. He was only what he appeared to be—a sniveling sneak thief. The fight had gone out of him.

After Evan had grabbed Saul's collar, we headed for the house—a dismal, silent group. Moth's screams for help were loud enough that they should have alerted everyone within a two-mile radius. But our ruckus had been lost in the chaos of another brewing storm.

This one was centered in Evan's yard. Lanterns were

lit. Two trucks sat in the drive with their motors running and their headlights on. But there was no rain to dampen the ill will from this storm. Anger, hurt, distrust, and hostility pelted everyone until we were spotted.

A stillness fell. A fist raised in anger froze in midair. Mouths hung open. Eyes were wide with surprise. It might have been comical, but I'd had my laugh for the evening.

Rosalie was on the porch with the younger children. I looked for Katie but didn't see her. Cleome and Edna faced Cecil. His fist was raised, his face twisted with rage. Sam Kramer and Eli Detweiler were squared off. The old bishop's shoulders were stiff and uncompromising. Sam, his scrawny neck wrapped in a brace, was busy situating his teeth.

My voice was droll. "Having a party and you didn't invite us?"

That broke the spell that held them. The shouting match took up where our interruption had stopped it. Cecil could be heard above everyone else.

He ranted, "Behind my back, Edna. You'd make me a laughingstock."

"We're friends," Edna tried to explain.

"Friends?" shouted Cecil. "You have plenty of friends without her."

"I saw you on my place today," Sam said to Detweiler.

"I admit to being there," replied the bishop.

"You're the one who's been letting my goat out," said

Sam. He crossed the yard to the animal. "Saul had better be okay." He ran a hand over the animal's wiry hair and glared at Detweiler. "You're trying to cause me trouble."

"And I'll continue to say, I am not."

"Then what the hell were you doing on my land?"

I shut out Cecil so I could hear Detweiler's answer.

The bishop said, "I've purchased some trees on the land that connects with your property. Instead of harnessing up the buggy, I walked over there. I've done it before, and you never said anything."

"That was before *she*"—here Sam dramatically pointed at me—"started coming around asking questions. The sheriff took me in for questioning. Said he found the murder weapon on my land. Then she dang near kilt me, ramming his car with hers, with me sitting locked in the backseat."

Cecil abandoned his argument with his wife to side with Sam. "Damned right," he shouted. "*She* came sneaking around my house while I was gone. Asking questions. Trying to get my wife to tell her where I was the night the Amish man died."

He took a step in my direction. "My business is my business. I thought I'd made that clear. If need be, I'll repeat it for you."

"Now, Cecil," began Edna.

He didn't let her finish. He jabbed the air with his finger. "I don't want to hear one word from you. I've seen and heard enough."

"If you've heard enough," said Cleome, "then you

know Edna and I were talking about our gardens."

"I don't give a damn if you were talking about the second coming of Christ. I don't want her talking about it with you."

Evan had given over the care of Saul to Sam so he was free to go to Cleome. He faced Cecil. "There will be no more meetings between my wife and yours. There will be nothing between us as neighbors. I'm asking you to leave."

Cecil stared at Evan. The Amish man stood his ground. For a brief moment, I thought I saw respect on Cecil's face. But if that unfamiliar emotion had been there at all, it didn't tarry. He scowled. "Let's go, Edna."

When Edna turned to obey her husband, it was more than I could stand.

"Go," I shouted, flapping my hands in the air. "Just climb meekly in that truck and toddle on home. I don't understand you people. Can't visit who you want. Can't grow flowers. Can't walk across someone's property." I shook my head and lowered my voice. "There was a time when neighbors helped neighbors. When ideas were exchanged. I don't expect you, Cecil, to accept Evan's way of life, but common courtesy is supposed to extend beyond all boundaries."

As I paused in my tirade, Detweiler said, "Them going their way, and us going ours, is right."

My eyes narrowed. "But neither of you are going anywhere. This is your home. You live within walking distance of each other. In the last few days, I've had the Bible quoted to me more times than I can count, from all kinds of people. What about 'love thy neighbor'? Or do you choose to honor only parts of the Bible? The ones that suit your purpose?"

"I don't expect you to understand," said Detweiler.

I threw up my hands in disgust. "You're right. I don't understand. All I see ahead for you is loneliness and sadness. If Edna and Cleome want to visit, what's the harm? Neither woman is out to convert the other. All they want is to talk."

"Edna has friends," said Cecil.

"So does Evan's Cleome," countered Detweiler.

"This is all very entertaining," said Moth, "but frankly, I've had enough. If you, sir," he directed his query to Cecil, "would be so kind as to give me a ride to my car, I'll be on my way to River City."

"Who the hell are you?" demanded Cecil, his eyes measuring Moth's worth.

The businessman's jeans were covered with mud. A large L-shaped tear in one pants leg revealed a garish white thigh. Part of his shirttail had come untucked and hung half in, half out. Completing his ensemble was the umbrella still dangling from the crook of his arm.

"I'm J. W. Moth, owner of River City Wholesale Floral Company. I'll pay you handsomely if you get me away from this asylum."

I'd had my say. In fact, I'd had my fill of the entire group. Wearily, I offered, "I'll take you to your car, but first, I want to tell Katie good-bye." I looked at Cleome. "Where is she?"

Cleome's face was blank. Luke and John were on the

steps. Rosalie was leaning against the railing, her arm around her daughter, Amelia.

The muscles in my throat squeezed shut. I could hardly speak. "Cleome, make sure Katie is all right."

Cleome looked to Evan. He looked at me, then jerked his head toward the house.

Cleome took a lantern and hurried inside. Breathlessly, I watched the light travel from room to room. My eyes were glued to the back door. I prayed Katie would step out on the porch with that special smile on her face.

But it was Cleome who opened the door. She came to Evan's side and took his arm in a tight grasp. "Katie's not here. She's not in the house."

"Evan, tell me what happened," I said firmly. "What did Katie say when she came to get you?"

"She said that you were in danger. That someone was in the field again, just like the night Isaac died."

"Oh, no," I breathed. "Who heard her say this? Who else was here?"

Evan frowned. "I don't see what that has to do with Katie being gone."

Pieces were falling into place. Horrible pieces that were turning my heart into a rough-edged chunk of ice. The killer knew Katie had seen someone the night Isaac was murdered.

The killer feared that Katie might recognize who that someone had been.

The killer had taken Katie.

And I knew who the killer was, but I needed Evan

to say the name aloud. "Who, Evan? Who was here?"

"Cleome wanted more tomatoes to make relish. Ours are just about through bearing—"

I wanted to pull my hair out. "Who was here, Evan?"

He blinked at me. "Don't get upset, Bretta. Since it rained, Katie may have gone down to the creek to—" He stopped when he saw the fire in my eyes. "It was Margaret. Margaret Jenkins. She's always willing to share the vegetables from her garden. She shares with everyone."

Chapter Twenty

Margaret's name didn't cause a ripple of suspicion among the group of people in Evan's yard. There wasn't time to explain, and I wasn't sure they'd believe me if I tried. I needed help. All I saw around me was malevolence.

I took a deep breath and stepped up to Cecil. Quietly, I told him to call Sid and send him to the Woodgrove Funeral Chapel. He listened, but his chin lowered until it rested on his chest. At the end, I offered a quiet, dignified, "Please do this. A life depends on it."

He didn't answer. There wasn't time to plead. There wasn't time to find a phone and call Sid myself. I'd wasted too many precious seconds already. I got in my car and drove away.

"Carl, you were right," I murmured, as I headed for Woodgrove. "It was so damned obvious. I should have seen it sooner." I cursed my stupidity and prayed that I wouldn't be too late.

I parked a block away from the funeral home, took my keys off their chain, and palmed the miniature flashlight—an item I usually consider too small to be useful.

I locked the car and stuffed the keys in my pocket. I tried the light to make sure it worked. It did.

I walked down the street, stalked the shadows, and mapped out my plan. I drew a shaky breath.

Katie.

She had to be safe. Would Margaret take the life of an innocent child?

An image of three boys killed on the curve of the road to Woodgrove flashed in my brain. An accident? Maybe. But tell that to three grieving mothers. Explain away parking on a road to steal an iron pipe to use as a murder weapon. Justify implicating an old man like Sam Kramer in the murder of Isaac, who had only wanted to grow flowers.

I built my courage on anger. Formed the foundation on injustice. By the time I reached the funeral home, I knew what I had to do.

If Cecil had made the call I'd requested, I could expect Sid or a deputy in about twenty minutes. In that time I had to make damned sure that I was right about Margaret's guilt. I immediately suppressed the thought of Cecil not cooperating. In my house of courage, I added a window of opportunity. I'd have to leave the sash up so I could crawl through.

I crept to the side door and peeked in.

Lights. People. Tears. Flowers.

The main slumber room was diagonally across from my hiding place. I slipped unnoticed in the door and waited for my chance to take the stairs up to the second floor.

It was seven-fifteen. Most visitations last an hour. I had time to search Margaret's apartment before the people left. If I could just get upstairs . . .

I craned my neck. Margaret was at the front door, bidding a couple good-bye. Her back was to me. I looked across the hall to the main slumber room. Only the closed casket. The name on the register: CLARENCE ENGELHART. My old friend.

On tiptoe I swung around the newel post and took to the carpeted steps. My heart pounded for those few seconds when I was in plain view. But once I'd made the bend and was out of sight, I leaned weakly against the wall and sucked a quivering breath into my lungs.

Thoughts flew fast and free in my head.

Margaret had tried to kill me.

Carl hadn't prepared me for this rush of adrenaline that torqued through my body.

Margaret had raised that winch too high, knowing it would let Mr. Engelhart fall. She'd counted on knocking me out, but I'd come around too quickly. If I hadn't, what would she have done then?

Another thought to squelch.

I took a step up and heard the rasp of my shoe on bare wood. The carpet ended at the turn of the staircase. Treading lightly, I worked my way up. At the top I flipped on the flashlight and guided its tiny beam around the room. It could have been inhabited by the Amish. Shades at the windows, no fancy drapes. Plain dark furniture. A kerosene lamp on a dresser. I tested a light switch and almost purred with satisfaction.

Nothing. She'd removed the bulbs. No pictures on the walls. The room was as unadorned as Margaret herself. Dark dress. Braids in the Amish tradition.

Margaret had said "our Lord" when she'd comforted the woman the day I'd reported Leray's murder. The use of that phrase should have alerted me, made me examine her involvement more closely, but I'd missed it. I'd allowed Margaret to guide me into believing that her speaking the Amish language and subscribing to the Amish magazine were because she didn't want to make a blunder when she dealt with them.

This room went beyond any desire to please. I knew, as sure as I was standing here, that she'd grown up Amish. But why had she renounced her beliefs?

I picked up my feet so they wouldn't scuff against the floor and went to her closet. I searched behind the dark clothes hoping to find Katie, but instead, I stirred up a soft, subtle scent that tickled my brain with its familiarity. I crossed the room to Margaret's dresser and eased open a drawer. Nestled under her cotton panties was a round box. The lid read PERFUMED BODY POWDER.

I experienced a flash of doubt. Perfume, scents of any kind, even deodorants are considered by the Amish to be too worldly. I reminded myself that Margaret was playing two roles. For the Woodgrove residents, she's Margaret Jenkins, modern funeral director and good friend. When she's alone, she lives the life of the Amish.

I reached for the box and heard Carl's voice rumble a warning, "Fingerprints, Bretta." I nodded and used a pair of Margaret's undies to cover my hand. I pried up the lid and saw cash. Four hundred-dollar bills, some twenties, and tens. Emergency money tucked away. Grimly, I put it back in the drawer and straightened the clothes.

Sid could make a comparison of this money with the packet of bills in my glove compartment. Would a residue of powder mark my bills as coming from this box?

If so, it was tied up. A done deal.

Katie.

I heard her name so plainly, at first I thought someone had spoken aloud. She was alive, I was sure of it. But she needed help. I made quick work of the few rooms upstairs. She wasn't there, but I did find a back staircase. I eased my way down it, then opened the door a crack into an eight-foot-wide corridor. Murmur of voices. I was close to the slumber room. I stepped out and looked around. Another door. It led to the basement.

I didn't hesitate. I took the steps rapidly, flashed my light at the concrete walls. Only a partial basement. Most of it was the garage. Boxes, empty. The hearse, zero. The family car. A wadded-up Kleenex on the floorboards. I put my ear to the trunk and rapped sharply. No response.

I was running out of places to look. All that remained was the ground floor. Where was Sid? Should I go outside and wait for him? I tried the doors. Locked; no bolt. I needed a key. I flashed my light at the exposed beams, looking for a nail and a key. Cobwebs. I could break a window, but someone might hear.

My only choice was to go back up a flight to the main floor. I didn't feel at risk until I was at the top, then I hurried down the short hall to a pair of double doors.

The showroom, or "selection room." Since the visitation was in progress, Margaret wouldn't need this room. I clicked the door open and had barely gotten inside when I heard her voice. She was so close my heart threatened to become an ornament on the outside of my shirt. I squeezed my eyes shut and waited.

"Here's the restroom, Mr. Sadler. Watch your step," Margaret cautioned.

I leaned weakly against the door. Suddenly, it was given a solid whack. My eyes binged open.

"What's in there?" asked a gruff old voice that I took to be Mr. Sadler's.

"I'd rather you didn't hit the door with your walker," admonished Margaret. "Here, let me show you."

I whirled to face the double doors. Which one was she going to open? Which one should I hide behind? I jumped behind the door on my left and watched it swing to within an inch of my nose.

"See," said Margaret, switching on the light. "This is the selection room. When you and your wife come by Monday, I'll be glad to show you everything. But right now I have to..."

There was a shuffling and a *klunk*. "Don't see the coffin that Clarence is laid out in."

"I have another just like it on order."

"When will it get here?" demanded the old fart. "I don't plan on needing it for a time. But at my age, who knows?"

"I'm sure you won't need it for years, Mr. Sadler, but to ease your mind, the bronze casket will arrive on Tuesday. Now here's the restroom. I have to go back to the front. Everyone is leaving."

I was plastered against the wall. My lungs screamed for oxygen. I was too scared to twitch, too scared to draw the slightest breath. Sweat gathered on my upper lip.

The lights went off. The door creaked shut. When the latch caught, I put as much distance as the room allowed between me and those doors.

Everyone was leaving? What time was it? A check of my watch told me it was a quarter till eight. Early for a visitation to end. Not much of a crowd for Mr. Engelhart.

Sid should be here any minute. As hard as I tried, I couldn't suppress my fear that Cecil hadn't called him. If I could find Katie, I'd leave, call Sid myself, and throw everything I had into his lap.

Find Katie. But where?

I snapped on my tiny flashlight and let its feeble glow travel the room. Margaret hadn't minded opening the door for Mr. Sadler. Did that mean there was nothing here?

The carpet softened my steps as I hurried from casket to casket. Each casket had two separate lids. The upper one was open, the bottom closed. Katie was small. Could she be tied and gagged? Her little body stuffed at the foot of one of these death boxes?

I shuddered.

At each casket, I reached under the drape that separated the head from the foot. All I found were the L-shaped handles and some papers explaining the virtues of the casket.

My emotional disposition moved from apprehension to bitter despair. My light picked up the muted hues of the purple casket that I'd admired the day I'd been here with Margaret.

The lid was closed.

She had said she was going to return it. I advanced with trepidation. What if Katie was dead?

"Shut up," I muttered through clenched teeth.

The lid wasn't entirely down. One of those L-shaped rods had been wedged under the seal to keep it from being airtight. I needed both hands. I gripped the end of the flashlight with my teeth and pushed my fingertips under the lid. Dread brought goosebumps to my arms. Blood thundered in my ears. I heard the heavy plunk as the rod fell to the floor. But I didn't give it a second thought. My eyes were on Katie.

I took the light out of my mouth and played it over her. She looked peaceful. Her clothing smoothed and arranged. Her hands clasped across her stomach. Her eyes closed. Her skin . . .

I licked my dry lips and put a trembling hand against the flesh of her cheeks.

Warm. Gloriously, deliciously alive and warm.

Tears welled up in my eyes and rolled over their rims. I blinked to clear my vision.

"Katie," I whispered urgently. "Wake up, honey."

She didn't move.

I put the light to her closed eyes and jostled her thin shoulder. "Katie," I said, more fiercely. "Wake up. Come on. Open your eyes."

Nothing.

I laid the flashlight on the curved lid of the casket, then I eased my hands under her unresponsive body. She was as limp as a flower left too long without water. Softly, I talked to her, trying to penetrate the dark recesses of her mind.

Drugs? Margaret had been a nurse before she'd become an—undertaker. I deliberately substituted this word for funeral director. The woman was a disgrace to her profession. A mockery of all the people who'd allowed her into their lives at a time when they were at their most vulnerable.

"Move your arms, Katie," I instructed. "Grab my neck. Help me," I implored her.

There was just the tiniest of response in her fingers.

"Wiggle your fingers again, honey."

She obeyed. I smiled. With renewed strength, I lifted her out of the box and laid her on the floor. I was bending over her, rubbing her hands, when I heard the showroom door open.

Every muscle in my body tightened protectively. I huddled over Katie and waited.

The flashlight!

I'd left it on top of the casket. I looked up. The beam had seemed so minute before. Now it looked like a searchlight as it pierced the gloom.

The ceiling lights flashed on. Footsteps. I turned my head, knowing what I'd see. Sometimes it can be deadly to be so damned right.

Margaret stood fifteen feet away. The expression in her eyes was fearsome, the trocar in her hand a wicked weapon.

Slowly, I rose so I could face her. I said, "Not a big crowd tonight. I guess Mr. Engelhart outlived most of his friends."

She ignored my distracting comments, waved the trocar at me. "Move." She pointed to the embalming-room doors. "Through there. You know the way."

"I really should pay my respects to Mr. Engelhart. We have a score to settle. I only concede round one."

Margaret's lips curled with a nasty smile. "Don't worry, my dear, you'll have all of eternity to get even."

In horror, I listened to her plans for me.

"... prick of a needle. A deep sleep," she was saying. "The Engelharts don't want to see Clarence again. The casket will be sealed." She raked me with a glance. "You're slim and trim. Your meddlesome body will tuck nicely in with his."

Icy fingers of fear touched the nape of my neck.

Buried alive!

I'd rather be stabbed, leave a pool of blood on her carpet. Evidence of foul play. Something for Sid to see if he ever came.

Margaret advanced a step and brandished the trocar at me. "Move," she ordered again.

"The sheriff will be here any minute." I pretended to look at my watch, but I stole a glance at Katie, lying unconscious on the floor. I smiled at Margaret with what I hoped she'd take as confidence. "Yeah. Any minute," I added for good measure.

"I doubt it. He called earlier and asked to speak to you. I told him I hadn't seen you." She paused, then added, "No one saw you come in here."

"My car—"

"Isn't parked anywhere close to the chapel. I checked."

"When?"

"When I saw the chandelier move in the main corridor."

"What? What does that have to do with anything?"

"These old houses have their own peculiarities. Someone walking across the floor upstairs makes the chandelier vibrate. Leon was going to get it fixed. When he died, and I was alone, it didn't matter anymore. No one walks up there when *I'm* down here."

"You as good as killed those boys, Margaret. You parked on that dangerous curve so you could steal that piece of pipe."

"If they'd been watching the road, they'd have seen my car. It was an unfortunate accident."

"You ordered the wreath. Paltry compensation for their young lives. What was your reasoning?"

"It seemed the right thing to do."

"And the snake in my car? Was that the right thing to do?"

She shuddered. "Everyone in town knows about that snake. Hodges talked about it all the time. Nasty thing. I wore gloves. Shoved it into a pillowcase." She glared at me. "I thought I had you when I knocked you out in the embalming room, but you came around too fast. You had to be stopped. I remembered Leray's snake when you talked about Moth's."

"How did you get it in my car?" I asked, moving closer to her so Katie would be behind me.

"I followed you all over town, waiting for the right moment. I'd just about given up when you parked on the curve. That was my sign. Our Lord took those boys at that place. I knew I was doing the right thing. When you parked there, you had to die."

Beads of sweat erupted on my forehead. Margaret spoke of murder so calmly. "You killed Hodges, too?"

She shrugged. "Nothing escaped that man's attention. He'd seen the parsnips growing in my garden and had asked for some. I'd put him off. When he started causing Rosalie trouble, he had to be stopped. It was simple to gather a few water hemlock roots when I gathered my weeds. Leray took the sack like the glutton he was."

"And Isaac?"

Margaret's jaw clenched stubbornly.

"Don't stop now," I said. "Or are you tired of talking? Want me to take over?"

"Shut up!" she hissed.

"You knew Isaac was antagonizing the council by

237

growing his flowers. I'm sure you thought you were helping to defuse the volatile situation when you let Sam's goat out of his pen. If this poor, dumb animal wrecked havoc, so be it, but bigger trouble was brewing, wasn't it?"

Margaret raised her chin defiantly, but she didn't speak. Slowly, I went on. Most of what I said was supposition, but Margaret didn't contradict me.

"The stakes were raised when the council discovered Isaac was propagating a mutation that had an impressive monetary value. Detweiler must have been enraged and outraged by Isaac's actions. That's when shunning was first mentioned, and you knew you had to do something."

I took another step toward her. It was dangerous closing the gap between us, but I wanted Katie as far away from us as possible. "I saw your apartment upstairs. You grew up Amish, didn't you? But something happened. You renounced their beliefs, became part of our modern society, but your roots are bound with these quiet, decent people."

I stopped, hoping she would fill in the rest. She stared at me unblinkingly. I took a deep breath and gathered my strength. "You worked it all out. The murder weapon. Isaac dead. Poor Rosalie. But her grief would heal. You see that all the time. You were sparing her, weren't you? To be shunned must have been a terrible experience."

My voice softened. "Who was shunned, Margaret? Was it someone in your family?"

She licked her lips. "My father put rubber tires on his farm wagon. The State Highway Department said his iron wheels were tearing up the blacktop road. Father was such a stickler about following the rules of our people. But on this one instance he didn't see that he had a choice. He begged the council to understand, but they refused. They told him to use the gravel roads, even though it would take him miles out of his way. Father was a stubborn man. He ruined my life and my mother's when he went against the council."

"You saw Isaac was heading for the same fate as your father. You knew what would happen to his family if he was shunned."

She didn't answer. I murmured, "What about Isaac's mutation? Did you kill it, too?"

"Yes."

"What did you do, Margaret?"

"I poured embalming fluid in the water tank."

Formaldehyde. So that's what I'd smelled in the greenhouse and in the embalming room. It had been on the towel Margaret was holding, supposedly to revive me. From the moment I'd followed her out of her office, I'd sealed my own fate.

"It's a killer," I whispered. "But then, so are you."

I sprang at the older woman. I aimed for her legs, hoping to topple her. I caught her unaware, but her reflexes were in prime condition. Her arm whipped around, and the trocar crashed into my head. Not as hard as she would have liked, but the blow left me dazed.

I sank to my knees. I saw a flash of movement and ducked. I felt the breeze of the weapon stir the hairs on my neck. I rolled across the carpet. My way was blocked by a cart holding a casket. I crawled around it and heard Margaret hot on my trail. Her breathing was ragged.

I struggled to my feet. Margaret was across from me, a lovely oak casket between us. The upper lid was open, the bottom closed. The air whistled as she made a swipe at my face with the trocar. I grabbed her arm when she made another pass in the opposite direction.

I was amazed at her strength. But then she'd built up her muscles moving bodies. I never lifted anything heavier than a vase of flowers. I doubled my efforts to overpower her. We wrestled across the curved bottom lid, seesawing back and forth. I'd gain ground, then lose it. I was on the viewing side of the casket. The brass fittings dug into my stomach. Margaret's fingernails raked my skin. But I kept my hold, and so did she.

Margaret's position was hampered by the upper lid. I used that to my advantage. She couldn't move around the end of the casket. I kept pulling her against the lid, pounding her arm against the wood, hoping she'd lose her hold on the trocar.

Suddenly, the wood splintered and the hinges gave way. The lid crashed to the floor. Margaret screeched. "My most expensive casket, and it's ruined!" Her eyes glittered anew with malice. Her teeth were clenched with rage. Swiftly, she reached across and grabbed a handful of my hair. At the same time she swatted at me with the trocar.

I screamed for Sid. I called for Carl. At some point, I even shouted for Mr. Engelhart to help me. This gave Margaret pause. I used that moment to get a better hold on her, and I pulled my hair from her grasp.

Abruptly, Margaret turned and looked down at the floor. Sternly, she said, "No, Katie. Stop."

It was a ploy I should have recognized. But Katie was my responsibility. I froze. Margaret had anticipated my reaction perfectly. Caught off guard, I lost my leverage. My feet left the floor. I was at Margaret's mercy, and she didn't have any to spare.

Inch by horrifying inch, she dragged me kicking and screaming toward the yawning bed of the casket. My body heaved and shuddered at this fate. I fought with every ounce of strength I had left, which wasn't much. I was a goner. Margaret only grew stronger, fired with determination to do me in. She bent over me. I saw the trocar rise.

Out of nowhere, another hand appeared. It gripped Margaret's arm in a firm grasp. In a droll voice, Sid said, "Boys, help the one in the casket. She sounds like she's still got some life left in her." He twisted Margaret's arm. The trocar clattered to the floor. "Meanwhile, I've got this one under control."

Epilogue

Once I was out of the casket and on my feet, I saw the room was full. Besides Sid and his men, there were Evan, Cleome, and Edna. Cleome was on her knees at her daughter's side. Tears streaked the Amish woman's face. Her voice was tender as she talked to Katie.

Katie's eyes were open. She looked confused, but she moved her lips. I couldn't understand what she was saying, but from the smile on Cleome's face, I assumed the child was coherent.

Edna fussed over me. She smoothed my hair, touched my cheek. She rambled on about what a brave woman I was. She told how Cecil had phoned Sid, but that he'd made my request for assistance sound like a joke. With Evan pressuring her, Edna had called Sid herself. She'd demanded that the sheriff go to the Woodgrove Funeral Chapel posthaste.

Evan. He stood just inside the door, his straw hat in his hands. Was he upset? Did he blame me in any way for the danger Katie had been in? I knew if that were the case, I'd be devastated. I cared what this man thought of me.

Slowly, I walked to him. I took a breath and said, "I guess it's over, Evan." Tears sprang to my eyes.

To my surprise, he wrapped his strong arms around me. With my nose buried in his chest, I smelled woodsmoke, fresh air, and sweat from a hardworking man.

I pulled away and smiled up at him. He gave my hair a tender stroke, then took his place at his wife's side. Cleome had witnessed our embrace. She reached for Evan's arm possessively and stared at me.

Click. Another piece fell into place.

Cleome was jealous of my friendship with Evan. I was sorry she felt that way. My interest in him, in both of them, was tied to the house they shared, and to the farm that had been a big part of my life. It would pain me; but if need be, I could cut that tie, leave their friendship, and carry on.

Perhaps Cleome realized it, too. She left Evan's side and came to me. She fumbled nervously with the fringe of her black shawl. Her words were spoken softly. "Thank you for taking care of our Katie, and for being a good friend. You are always welcome at our house."

I could see the words weren't easy for Cleome to say. I nodded, then turned to Sid.

He asked if I needed a ride home. I said no. We agreed that I would give my statement in the morning. Right now all I wanted was a shower and bed.

I don't remember the drive to River City, but I must have done it. Obvious. I was sitting in my garage. I folded my arms across the steering wheel and gave up all pretense. No one would witness my desolation.

I cried at my fears, at life in general, at death that was so specific. I sobbed because I was alone. Because Carl was only a voice in my head and not a warm body for me to be cradled against.

When the storm of my weeping was over, I dragged myself from the car and into the house. I roamed restlessly for a time, going from room to room but still avoiding the master bedroom suite. I was on my fourth trip down the hall when I came to an abrupt halt at the door. I'd fought for my life tonight when I'd grappled with Margaret across that oak casket. Did I have the inner strength to fight for my own peace of mind? Could I let Carl go?

My fingers trembled as I turned the key, and the door creaked open. Undisturbed dust, mustiness, and just a faint hint of Carl's Old Spice aftershave lotion wafted to my nose. My stomach muscles cramped at the flood of memories.

Everything was the same. No one, not even me, had crossed this threshold since I'd moved my possessions out the day after Carl died. The bed was as I'd left it— as the paramedics had left it when they'd taken Carl's body away.

The sheets, blankets, and coverlet were hanging over the footboard. I stared at the bed. In my mind, I relived our lovemaking. Once again, I felt Carl's hands on my body. Felt the warmth of his touch. Saw the glow of passion in his eyes.

I heard a strange, mournful moan and realized it came from my own throat. I thought I'd cried all the tears that I had, but I was wrong. They streamed down my face. Carl had loved me so much. He'd shown me his love often. On our last night together, I'd turned over on my side and gone to sleep, blissfully happy.

He'd turned over and died.

Everywhere I looked, I saw him. Leaning against the headboard of our bed. Combing his hair at the mirror. Tossing his dirty clothes onto the floor by the bureau.

"How could I sleep when you lay dying?" I asked aloud. "Why didn't I know? Why didn't I wake up? Why didn't I sense you needed me?"

I'd awakened and found his body as cold and lifeless as this room was tonight. I dashed a hand across my eyes and turned away. I left the room, but this time I didn't close the door.

Maybe I needed a change. I'd keep the flower shop. It was my rock. But maybe it was time to sell this house and find a place that didn't have so many heart-wrenching memories. Carl's life insurance money was sitting in the bank gathering interest. Before now, I couldn't bare to touch a cent of it.

The idea of a bed-and-breakfast appealed to me. I'd hire a manager. My heart fluttered hopefully. Was I onto something? I'd have people around me, but more important, I wouldn't have to come home to an empty house.

An image of the Beauchamp mansion flashed in my brain. When Carl and I were first married, we'd dreamed about someday owning a house like it. In those days it had been a pipe dream. But what if . . .

I'd heard the Beauchamp estate was for sale. Who had it listed?

The newspaper.

I opened the door and nearly stepped on it. A smile wavered at the corner of my lips. A pink carnation wrapped in tissue lay on top. I pulled the card from the envelope and read:

Dear Bretta:

Accept this flower as a token of my gratitude. I was joking when I first said you're as wise as Solomon. Now, I know it's true. Your wisdom in dealing with Jamie has put a gleam of determination in her young eyes. I know we have some rough roads ahead, but for now, thank you.

Bill Fenton

The glacier around my heart began to thaw. Then I took another look at the envelope. "Pick a Posie."

"Allison Thorpe!" I muttered. "I've got to put some of this Solomon wisdom to use. What I need is a blockbuster ad campaign. I'll be damned if I let *that woman* get ahead of me."